Strong Deaf

STRONG DEAF

Lynn McElfresh

South Hampton, New Hampshire

LCCN: 2011937645

ISBN: 978-1-60898-126-7 (hardcover : alk. paper)
ISBN: 978-1-60898-127-4 (pbk. : alk. paper)
ISBN: 978-1-60898-128-1 (ebk.)

www.namelos.com

To my husband, Gary, the best short-order cook,
travel companion, and first reader ever.
You make our life together a joyful adventure.

JADE—I pushed through the door as the clock chimed three. They should be getting back soon.

"Beezley! Wanna go out?"

Beezley didn't even twitch, just went right on sleeping.

I knelt down next to Beezley, buried my face in his neck, and whispered in his ear. Beezley almost woke up. His tail thumped once before he drifted back to doggie dreams.

Two minutes later Beezley struggled to his feet and wobbled to the door. I looked out, but there was no car coming down the street. Then Beezley started tap-dancing, his toenails clicking on the tile foyer as he shifted his weight from foot to foot.

I didn't see or hear a car coming down the street. I knew Beezley didn't see or hear anything either, but somehow Beezley knew. Marla was almost here.

Beezley let out a little yowl. I looked up. I saw our SUV come around the corner. The dog that could barely move a few minutes ago was about to jump through the screen door. My first instinct was to close the front door and lock it. But Beezley would have none of that. He wanted out, and he wanted it right now.

Dad had asked me if I wanted to go with him when he picked up Marla from school. He tried to bribe me with lunch at McDonald's on the way there and a stop at Baskin-Robbins on the way back. Baskin-Robbins was really tempting, but I said no. I'd already wasted hours of my life on the road between our house in Middleton and Marla's school in Bradington.

Instead, I met Tana at the park and we practiced catching grounders. She hit to me and then I hit to her. I'm getting better, I think. Hope so. Practice starts next week. I'm going to make first string this year—I just know it!

A low, impatient grumble came from Beezley as he watched the SUV pull into the driveway. It wasn't a growl or a moan, but sort of a mix between the two. Beezley looked up at me, his eyes pleading with me to open the door.

Beezley stopped chasing squirrels years ago. Now he waddles and moves slowly. But when I opened the door, he galloped down the steps and across the yard. Straight to Marla.

Marla had her back to him as she pulled boxes from the back seat of the SUV. She didn't even see him coming. When she felt him behind her, Marla turned and fell to her knees. Beezley covered her face with doggie kisses. This happens every time Marla comes home, which, thankfully, isn't all that often.

I don't know why I followed Beezley into the driveway. I should have gone straight to my room and shut the door.

Marla opened her eyes and made a face when she saw me. "What wrong?" she signed.

"Dog kiss stink," I signed back.

She signed to Dad that I looked like I'd been eating lemons because I had a sour face. She had her back turned slightly to me and her hand low, like she was being nicey-nice. She didn't know I could see what she was saying.

I walked back to the house.

I heard my sister's deaf voice. She uses her voice only when she's excited. Even then it's not understandable. I looked back over my shoulder to see what she was excited about.

"Why Jade run away? Why not help?" I saw her sign to Dad.

I trotted up the steps and slammed the door. But no one heard. Not even Beezley.

I hate summer vacation.

marla—Open car door, climb out, stretch. Home long time. All summer. No homework. No tests. No dorm inspection.

Surprise. Feeling same snake touch leg. Maybe scream, but no. Turn around, Beezley greet me. Not snake. Dog tail. Beezley my dog. Sister Jade think Beezley her dog, because Jade live home all year. I older. I first daughter. First love of Beezley.

Beezley now old. Gray nose. Hug Beezley neck, shut eye. Beezley lick face. Laugh. Dog tongue tickle. Open eye. Jade face surprise me. Very angry. "What wrong?"

"Dog kiss stink," Jade sign. Jade run away. No help.

Beezley kiss more. Laugh more. Jade jealous. Now I home, Beezley sleep my bed, not Jade bed.

JADE—My eyes popped open just as the sun rose above the horizon, which in mid-June is at 5:56. WRGM would be playing the morning mystery song in just four minutes. I love WRGM. It's part of my morning routine. I reached over and clicked on the radio.

. . . I don't wear an S upon my chest.

Oh! My favorite! Argento's new hit "I'm No Hero." I stuck my feet straight in the air and kicked wildly, then jumped to my feet. Socks! I needed socks. *"Can't turn back time though I wish I could,"* I sang as I grabbed a pair out of my top drawer. I kept singing as I pulled them on, grabbed an extra rolled-up pair from the drawer for my improvised mic, and turned the radio up another notch just in time for the refrain.

"I'm no he-e-e-e-errrrrr-rooooooo . . ." I sang loudly as I slid

across the wooden floor, then added softly, almost in a whisper along with the lead singer, *"But maybe I am."*

It was a routine Tana and I had worked out at a sleepover at her house.

"I don't have myself two identities . . ." I threw my head back and sang out loud and proud. Then threw my head forward and shook my hair. Jazz hands as I sang out the next part. *"My girlfriend's name ain't Lois Lane . . ."* Big breath for the refrain, *"I'm no he-e-e-e-errrrrr-rooooooo . . ."* Again I slid across the floor.

Tana doesn't have wooden floors in her room, so we had to go to her tiled basement to do the sliding.

The next verse was fun and involved what Tana and I called high-stepping. Tana's kicks are way over my head. But she's a lot taller than I am. Everyone is.

I was into the third rep of the refrain, sliding, when Marla pushed through the door. I smacked right into her, which didn't improve the look on her face. Boy, did she look mad!

"Stop!" Her signs were big and coming fast and furious. "Wake me! Rude! Stop! Stop now!"

"Leave! My room!" I signed, then turned my back on her. *"I can't save you, I can't save me. Won't someone save us all?"* I sang into my sock.

Marla knocked the sock microphone out of my hand before I could add the *I'm no hero.*

This was too much. Too much!

I pushed past my crazed sister and raced for my parents' room. Marla followed me. I opened the door and marched to the foot of my parents' bed. The covers were pushed back from Mom's side of the bed, and I could see the indentation her head had made in the pillow. She was up already. Maybe she left early for work again. Dad was still asleep, lying on his back with his mouth open, snoring loudly. Dad's snoring is one reason why our rooms are at opposite ends of the house.

With both hands I pushed down on the foot of the bed and shook him awake. He sat straight up and his eyes fluttered open. He smacked his lips together a couple of times before wetting his dry lips with his tongue. His eyes had a wild, panicked look to them. He blinked hard a couple of times before he was able to focus on me at the foot of the bed.

"Marla in my room. Private. She needs to stay out," I signed.

His eyes shifted from me to Marla, who was standing right behind me signing wildly. I had no idea what she was saying.

Dad groaned and fell back on the bed.

I pushed down on the foot of the bed to get his attention again. "Marla not respect my private room," I signed when he looked up at me. "Tell Marla stay out."

From behind me I could hear the pop of Marla's lips as she mouthed words. She must have been excited, because as she signed I could hear her arms windmilling. I didn't look. I didn't care what she was saying. She'd barged into my room. *I* was the one whose privacy was invaded.

Dad put out his hand—a plea for both of us to stop signing. "Early," he signed, pointing to the clock. "Wait. Better time, not early."

"Marla start. Tell Marla." I didn't wait for a response. I turned, pushed past Marla, and rushed back to my room. I slammed the door.

I pushed my desk chair under the doorknob, hoping it would

wedge there. It wasn't heavy enough to keep Marla from coming in, but it would slow her down a little. I flopped on the bed, reached for the radio on the nightstand, and cranked up the volume. What did she care how loud my radio was? She's deaf!

Another song was playing. I'd missed the end of "I'm No Hero." The grand finale! My favorite part! And I'd missed the announcement of the song of the morning.

It was the first week of my summer vacation, and already it was ruined. All because of Marla.

marla—Jade run away like rat. Feel boom. Maybe Jade door.

Father close eye. Want sleep. I want same sleep. But sleep not happen because rude Jade.

No shake bed same Jade. Use quiet power. Cross arms, stare Father.

Eye have power. Father feel stare. Father open eye.

Sad eye. Disappoint because see me next to bed. No want disappoint Father. Only make anger grow.

"Early, Marla. Go sleep. Talk later." Father close eye. No look face.

Again, no shake bed. Shake like shout. Shake rude. Jade rude.

Eye look Father. Power eye. Power stare.

Father eye open, sit, sign, "What?"

"No sleep! Room like earthquake. All thing shake! Come see!"

I go my room. Look back. Prove Father follow.

Jade door have new sign:

KEEP OUT!

Baby writing under:

THAT MEANS YOU MARLA!

Point to door. Father see, but face show not patient. Father think fight between sisters baby fight. Father not understand. Jade baby one, not me.

Beezley sleep on bed. My bed near Jade room wall.

"What problem? Beezley sleep."

"Beezley sleep while world explode."

Put hand on wall share with Jade room. Ask Father do same.

Wall feel alive under hand. Feeling like something want break through. That something Jade music.

"Feel? Earthquake music wake me. Wall shake. Bed shake."

"Maybe move bed not next wall."

Stop. Think Father idea. Then toy bear fall from shelf over bed. Land on pillow.

"See!"

Father nod. Tap forehead. Father think hard. "Maybe move bed other wall."

Patience disappear. Sign big. "Not right. Why change room? Work hard past summer. Room perfect. Like. Love. Jade need considerate. Jade rude. Jade baby! Always Jade way."

Father put out hands. Meaning: Stop, wait. "No think now. Sleep now. Talk later. Sleep couch. Sleep guestroom."

Father go sleep.

Feel floor move. Feel Jade dance. No sleep guestroom. No couch. Want my room. All year share room with two girls. Now home. Now my room. Stay my room. Jade not make move.

Pull bed from wall. Try sleep. Father right. Bed not near wall better. Almost sleep, then two more bear fall. Hit head. This war.

JADE—After lunch, I met Tana at the park down the street. We ran for the swings.

I sat on a swing, pushed off, pumped hard, and swung so high that the chains went slack and it felt like I was falling. Then the chains caught, the swing jerked, and I was pulled backward through the air.

"She hasn't even been home twenty-four hours yet and already there are new rules," I told Tana. "Everything has to change because Marla's home. I wish she'd just stay at Bradington all year."

"So what are the new rules?"

I dragged my foot and came to a stop. My foot stirred up a little cloud of dust from the dirt patch under the swing, and I choked a little. "I can't turn on my radio until after eleven in the morning. Eleven."

Tana shrugged. "So you listen to your iPod instead."

"But I miss the whole morning program on WRGM."

Tana nodded.

"Not only can't I listen to the radio in the morning, but no dancing."

"No dancing?"

"Can you believe it?" I stood up, took two steps back, and pushed off, letting my feet poke high in the air straight in front of me.

"How does dancing bother Marla?"

"Get this! She claims she can feel me dancing from her room and it wakes her up."

"She feels your dancing?"

"She says it feels like her room is next to a horse barn."

"Horse? She called you a horse? By the way, what's the sign for horse?"

I signed horse for her.

"I'd sign horse like this . . . like I'm riding a horse." Tana jumped from the swing and galloped around a bit, holding imaginary reins in one hand and slapping the rump of her imaginary horse with the other.

I shrugged.

"Wow! She must be pretty sensitive if she can feel you dancing in the next room."

"You have no idea! Marla has 'Princess and the Pea' Syndrome. When Princess Marla is home, the whole house has to be rearranged for her convenience. For her comfort."

"So did Beezley sleep on her bed last night?" Tana started swinging again.

I nodded. I wished I'd never said anything to Tana about Beezley.

Beezley is old. Older than I am. Marla likes to tell how Beezley always slept by her crib. How he protected her and watched over her when she was a baby.

I'd told Tana—two years ago—that when Marla is at school, Beezley is my dog. He sits by me, sleeps by me, runs to me when I come through the door, but as soon as Marla comes home from school, it's as if I don't exist. I can't believe Tana remembers that conversation.

I don't know what's worse—having Beezley ignore me when Marla's around or having Tana remind me that Beezley ignores me when Marla's around. I wish Tana would forget. And I wish Marla would stay at Bradington.

"Yeah, Beezley farts all the time now. Bet Marla's room really stinks. Pretty soon she'll make a rule that Beezley can't sleep on her bed anymore unless he stops farting."

I pushed off hard, and as the swing reached its highest point, I jumped. I landed on my feet, but my momentum made it hard for me to come to a stop. I staggered forward a couple of steps and almost fell. I regained my balance, stopped, and turned toward Tana, who was still swinging.

I pulled an imaginary scroll from my back pocket and pretended to unroll it. I cleared my throat and used my best royal voice. "Hear ye! Hear ye! Princess Marla has decreed. All farting shall stop in the realm."

marla—Text school friend about earthquake music, elephant dance. At breakfast, tell Father that Jade like horse, but decide elephant more right. *Like live at circus*, I text friend.

Two roommate from Bradington, Jasmine, Tabitha, stay home alone when parents work. Not same me. Father computer worker. Work home summer because Jade baby. Need babysitter.

Father home all summer make me feel same baby.

Light in hall go on, off. Time for dinner. I text goodbye.

Walk stair. Bad smell attack me.

Smell grow near kitchen. Bigger. Bigger.

Know before see. Know smell. Hate smell. Smell is fish.

See fish on table. Jade, Father wait.

Close nose with fingers.

Father face show surprise. "What wrong?"

"Hate fish."

Father hit head. "Forget."

Father never remember.

Jade smile. Jade know. Jade plan. Purpose: mean.

Tell Jade, "No like fish. Make different food."

"Not a restaurant," Jade says. "Make yourself."

"No! Your job cook. You know I have hate for fish. You cook different."

"Maybe eat fish. Good," Father sign. Smile big. Rub stomach.

I frown. Jade smile more.

"Hate fish," I tell Father. "School many choice."

"Maybe you should go back to school," Jade say.

Father look Jade. Face show disapprove. Shake head. "Sisters must live happy together."

"Yes," I sign to Father, then look Jade. "Make happy now. Your job cook. Make different food now."

"I cook. See?" Jade point to fish on fork.

Jade eat. Yuck! Jade eat smell.

"You cook food I like now!" I pull back Jade chair.

Father wave hand to stop. "Marla, maybe eat sandwich."

Hunger grow. Stomach complain. I approve plan. "Sandwich fine. Jade make."

Jade move chair close to table, hug plate. "I'm eating. Make your own sandwich."

I turn to Father. "Jade job cook!"

"I cook! See?" Jade point to food on table. "What's your job? Complaining? You do your job good!"

Anger burn like fire. I no talk Jade. Jade no want help me. Jade want problem. I turn back to Jade and tell Father, "My job iron. My iron bad, I iron again. Jade no do my job."

"We forget you not like fish."

"*You* forget. Jade know."

I look Jade. Face show play surprise.

"Lie," I sign. "Face lie."

Jade smile. Smile make anger flame hot.

"Hungry now," I tell Father. "Fish smell. Maybe vomit." I open cabinet, take first box. Leave kitchen, go room.

Anger push me upstairs to room. Close door. Not close door with boom. Boom for baby same Jade. Lie bed. No open school box. Think about mean Jade. When Mother home, more understand. Wish Mother home now.

Mother work university science library. Work big project. Go early. Work late. Hope project finish soon. Need Mother home. Mother know Jade act with mean purpose. Father easy fooled. Father no understand.

Stomach complain again. Hungry. Look at box in hand. No! Oatmeal.

JADE—I thought I'd pee my pants when Marla grabbed a box of Quaker Instant Oatmeal from the pantry and ran from the room. Instant oatmeal! Yeah! Like she's going to munch on that. I laughed so hard, I shook all over.

Dad tapped my elbow. I looked up to see him shaking his head. I tried to look serious.

"Sister need together. Family important. Tana friend now, but maybe not twenty year future."

I took a sip of milk and tried to catch my breath. Dad was still staring at me. He was serious, so I tried to listen to him.

"I lucky have brother. Friends, not like brother. Friends here, but maybe not here. Brother always help me. Brother, family, important."

I nodded and took another bite of fish. I didn't think my relationship with Marla would ever be like Dad's relationship with Uncle Andrew.

From upstairs came a loud, angry bellow. It sort of sounded like a sick cow. I almost spit chewed-up fish across the table. I swallowed quickly, washing it down with a sip of milk. Luckily, Dad was bent over his plate eating and didn't notice. The bellowing continued. I had to take my plate to the sink so Dad couldn't see that I was about to die from laughter. I heard something hit the wall upstairs.

marla—Weekend arrive. Mother finish big project. World better now.

Mother plan big house clean. Attack dirt. Vacuum long rug in upstairs hall. When young, Beezley not like vacuum. Run, hide. Now Beezley sleep on my bed not knowing. Now Beezley deaf same me. Love for Beezley grow. Deaf gain.

Mother look my bedroom. Surprise show face. Mother point school box. "Why full? Why not empty?"

"No time," I sign. Turn back. Pat Beezley.

Mother tap floor with foot. Look, see Mother. "Lie! Home one week! Much time."

Face grow red. Sit on bed. Pat sleeping Beezley. No look Mother.

Mother tap shoulder. "What wrong? Not true you."

Mother not say more, but look at Jade room wall. Know Mother meaning. My room same Jade room now. Not order. Lazy.

Mother face show understand. Small smile. "Understand. Father easy. Mother not home, house grow wild."

I smile. "I teen now. Teen need sleep late! Magazine say true."

Mother face show not believe. "Sleep all day?"

I sign no. Remember first morning earthquake music. "First week, much sleep, but also ride bike, go ice cream, watch movie."

"Summer not for lazy."

"You go Bradington. Remember room inspection? Remember schedule? Remember all time have plan?"

Mother smile. Mother remember. "First week freedom. Second week work. Empty school box. Make room neat. Softball start fast."

JADE—I swear I've spent half of my life on this road. Every Friday, rain, snow, or suffocating heat, we drive two and a half hours to Bradington, where Marla goes to residential school for the deaf. I can't read in the car. It makes me sick to my stomach. I can't even play video games. Sometimes I listen to my iPod, but mostly I sleep. Just thinking about getting in a car makes me doze off.

I would never admit it to Marla, but I love my sister's school. The buildings are surrounded by huge trees and a big green lawn, behind a tall, fancy iron gate. And her dorm is an old brick mansion that looks like something out of a Disney movie.

Marla started going to Bradington when she was six years old. I missed her so much! I was four, in preschool then, and counting the years. After kindergarten I would go to Bradington just like Marla. Two more years. *Two more years!*

I wanted to live in a dorm like Marla did. I wanted to sit in the old dining hall and have wonderful meals cooked by Miss Kitchner and the friendly kitchen ladies. I wanted to be able to visit Grandmother and Grandfather for dinner once or twice a week.

On our trip home one Sunday evening, I tapped Mom on the shoulder and she turned around to look at me. I told Mom that when I went to Bradington, I hoped I would get to stay on the fourth floor just like Marla. The fourth floor, the top floor, had gabled windows and slanting ceilings. There were three girls to a room. Each girl had her own bed and dresser. Marla and her roommates shopped together that year, so they all had matching bedspreads.

"I want a purple bedspread," I told Mom. "And my roommates will all have purple bedspreads too."

I loved purple when I was little. I wore purple all the time. Everything I had was purple.

Mom looked at me like I was crazy. "Silly," she signed. "You no go Bradington. You not deaf."

I didn't say another word the rest of the trip home, but I felt my mom's signed words over and over. "Silly. You not deaf."

Of course I knew I could hear, but what did that have to do with anything?

Maybe Mom misunderstood what I was trying to say. That happens a lot. I have one shot with her. If I don't get my point across the first time, I'm dismissed.

So before we left Bradington the next week, I said the same thing to Dad. His eyes got sad like when the heater went out in our aquarium and all the fish died and he was the one to tell us girls.

"Bradington school for deaf," he signed.

"But I want to go. Bradington fun," I signed back to him.

"Your school fun, too," Dad signed. "You see."

Dad gave me a big hug. It's like he knew my school wouldn't be fun and he was trying to comfort me.

All the way home that week, I tried to plug my ears. But no matter how hard I tried to block the sounds out, I could hear my breathing, the hum of the tires. I didn't think it was fair that I should be punished because I could hear.

Going to Bradington was never the same after that. I still liked to go to Bradington, and I loved seeing my grandparents every weekend, but it was never the same.

I don't know what made me think about all that on our way to Bradington's 75th Anniversary, but as I dozed off, I was imagining that I had pretended to be deaf and been sent to Bradington.

Could I have pulled that off? Pretended to be deaf?

I might have fooled hearing people, but I doubted I could fool deaf people. My signing is good, but deaf people word things so differently. While my signs are more Exact Signed English, they use ASL, sort of a sign language shortcut, and even though I've been around it all my life I can never keep up with all the new signs and shortcuts they use. The word order they use is backwards and weird. We may look the same, but I think deaf people would know in a minute that I can hear.

I didn't think about these things for too long. Ten minutes into our trip and I was asleep.

marla —Go Bradington all weekend. Big anniversary. Seventy-five years. Very exciting.

Pack SUV. Beezley need ramp. Help Beezley walk ramp. Put blanket in dog box for Beezley comfort.

Long time travel. Father drive. Jade sleep. Much time for talking. Tell Mother about first week summer vacation. Tell about earthquake music. Tell about elephant dance. Tell about fish for dinner. No tell about oatmeal.

Mother nod. Mother agree Father no understand.

"Next week better," Mother signed. "I home dinner. No fish. Next week you, Jade play baseball. Attention for playing, not fighting."

Maybe. Excite to see other baseball girl, but Jade annoy. Jade like mosquito.

Mother wave hand for attention. "When I Bradington student, summer vacation different. Only me, parents. No sister. No brother. No deaf children. No summer sport play. Summer lonely. Live house all hearing. No deaf. Count days must have before return to school. Summer long."

"No summer sports. What for?"

"Maybe Mother think girl not play sport. Maybe Mother think deaf not play with hearing. Don't know."

"What doing all summer?"

"Read. Go library. Read two, three book every week."

I nod. "Maybe why you librarian now."

Mother nod. "Always love library. Library home."

Mother look at road. I look out window. Many farms. Horses. Cows. Trees. Barns.

Have secret wish. Guilty wish. Love parents, but have same wish to stay at Bradington all year. No want tell Mother I count days. Calendar hide under bed. Every night make X. Every night count how many days before return Bradington. Return friends. Return all deaf.

JADE—I can't believe I didn't wake up when we stopped at my grandparents' house to leave Beezley. I was still zonked out as Dad pulled into the parking lot at Bradington.

Dad opened my door and shook me awake.

I looked up expecting to see my grandparents' two-story house and felt confused when it wasn't.

"Wake up!" Dad signed to me as he shook me again. "Dinner start fast."

I was half-asleep, groggy until Marla slammed her door and headed for the gymnasium entrance. I tried to get out of the SUV but realized I still had my seatbelt on.

Dad laughed and unclipped my seatbelt for me. Mom was headed toward the gym entrance, well behind Marla, and in a hurry to catch up when she turned and looked at me. Dad and I were way behind.

"Ahhhhhhhh," Mom called loudly.

I jumped at the awkward, abrasive sound and then looked around. At least no one was staring at us like at the grocery store back home. Here, either that sound wasn't heard or it was understood as a normal deaf voice.

"What?" I mouthed, throwing my hands up into the air for added emphasis.

Mom signed, "Hair ugly. Have pride!"

I stopped and looked in the side mirror of some car and saw that I had a bad case of bed head. Mom reached in her purse for a brush. She wanted to brush it for me, but she was in a hurry. That could mean only one thing: she'd yank too hard.

"No, myself," I signed, then held out my hand.

Reluctantly she handed the brush over. "Hurry. No late," Mom signed more to Dad than to me.

Mom was wearing nail polish. I couldn't remember the last time she put on nail polish. She had changed her clothes three times before she found just the right outfit. She was clearly very excited about seeing everyone here.

Dad waited for me as I brushed my hair. The side mirror wasn't giving me a clear view of myself, so I looked at Dad. I didn't say or sign anything, but my eyes asked if I looked okay.

"Look fine. *Beautiful,*" he said with an exaggerated gesture. "Mom not want late."

As soon as Dad and I came through the door, I saw Marla with her two roommates: Tabitha, a tall, thin black girl, and Jasmine, a much shorter Asian American. The three of them have been roommates forever. A couple of years ago, I made some joke about them being like Charlie's Angels.

Marla's face twisted in confusion. "What mean?"

"You know, like the movie *Charlie's Angels.* One white girl, one black girl, one Asian girl."

Marla blinked hard. "Never think different. All same. All deaf."

I thought of them as the Angels after that, no matter what Marla thought.

Her roommates are both cute, but Marla is beautiful. I got a strange twang of pride watching my sister from across the room. At home she's so bossy and annoying. But here, she stands out in a crowd.

I'm the shortest girl in my class. Marla is tall.

My hair is mousy brown; Marla's hair is a dark chestnut. My hair is thin and straight, very susceptible to bed head. In the morning it sticks out in all directions like doll hair. Marla's hair is thick and wavy and always looks perfect the moment she jumps out of bed in the morning.

My eyes are small and blue-gray. Marla's eyes are large and round and look like melted chocolate.

Marla has a wonderful smile. It lights up her face. It lights up the whole room.

My mouth is small. My lips are thin and tight. My lips are as pale as my face.

I watched Marla talking with her roommates. They were standing in a tight circle signing away to each other. There seemed to be a bubble of light around them. A special energy. I stood there for a minute, staring. Then I started to wonder what they were talking about. Marla had been text-messaging Tabitha and Jasmine fifteen times a day since she got home for the summer. What was left to say?

The gym had been decorated with the school colors, purple and gold. The place was packed, but it was oddly quiet for a crowded gym. Most people were signing, though there was a low murmur of conversation from hearing parents of current students.

Mom told me earlier that we were at Table 23. I found our table in the corner of the room and was about to sit down when someone tapped my shoulder. It was my Uncle Andrew. He hugged me so hard my feet left the ground.

"Short like mother family. Like tiny doll."

It took me a moment before I realized that the tall guys standing behind my uncle were my cousins, Derek and Dillon. I hadn't seen them since Christmas, almost six months, and I couldn't believe how tall they'd grown. Both were taller than their father. I swear they were each about five inches taller. They looked very grown up. They were wearing suits and looked like J. Crew models. I had never thought of my cousins as handsome before.

Each signed hello and hugged me. Being so close to them made me blush.

I looked up to see Marla signing to Jasmine and Tabitha. Even though they were halfway across the gym, I could see what they were saying.

"Yes! My cousins! You remember. Went to school here Bradington."

"More tall now," Jasmine signed.

"More beautiful now," Tabitha signed.

"Like prince."

"Prince C-H-A-R-M-I-N-G."

Tabitha was pushing Marla ahead of her. "Want meet again. Hurry."

"Now?"

"Yes! Now!"

The three started to weave their way through the crowded gymnasium but stopped when a big drum at the front table boomed.

All eyes turned toward the podium where my grandfather stood. He signed, asking everyone to find their tables and sit down.

marla—Drum boom. Meaning: Sit down. All people in room move.

"Want meet cousins. Not forget," Tabitha tell me. Her family sit Table 16. Left room side. Tabitha move different way.

Jasmine follow me. Her table close. But soon sit.

Many people sit before I arrive table. Gilbert family take all eight chair at Table 23. Four adult. Four children. But Derek, Dillon no look same children now. Look adult. I hope sit best chair between Derek, Dillon. Unhappy because Jade sit best chair. Empty chair between Aunt Kelly, Mother.

Uncle Andrew, Aunt Kelly sign hello. Drum boom again. All eye look front. I sit.

Ernie Gilbert walk proud to podium. Student, family see important man. See headmaster. I see Grandfather. Feeling of pride grow in chest. I sit tall. Must look important, because Grandfather important. Make Grandfather pride in me, same my pride in Grandfather.

Grandfather welcome alumni, welcome student, welcome family. Look around room. Other table of older people, student from Bradington long ago. Speech teacher, Mr. Hendley, interpret because many hearing. Most hearing people here family for current student. Mr. Hendley stand end of long table. See mouth move. Mr. Hendley talk into microphone. Grandfather not need microphone. Big screen behind Grandfather have TV picture of Grandfather signing, so all can see sign and face.

Yesterday Father say secret. Soon Grandfather show old picture. Many old picture. Football picture when Father student. Uncle Andrew picture when football player also. Mother picture when lacrosse player, cheerleader. Mother not know. Father demand promise not tell.

Now time for eat. See picture after food.

JADE—Marla made a face when she got to the table and saw that I snagged the best seat right between our hunky cousins. Derek is a college freshman this year. Dillon is a junior. And here I am, Jade Gilbert, sitting between two hot college guys.

They both go to Gallaudet, the only university for the deaf in the United States. My grandparents went there. My parents went there. Aunt Kelly and Uncle Andrew went there. Now Derek and Dillon are going there. I guess someday Marla will go there. It's another family tradition that doesn't include me.

Because it is the only university for the deaf, there are students from all over the country. On their breaks from school, Derek and Dillon visit their new friends. They fly lots of places. They took a trip to California on spring break, where they learned to surf! Derek was telling me about a really big wave and wipeout when the huge bass drum boomed again to get everyone's attention. You didn't have to hear it. You could feel the vibrations deep within your chest.

Everyone turned to look at the podium. After my grandfather welcomed us all, waiters came out and served a yummy dinner.

After dinner, there were speeches. Derek and Dillon turned their chairs so they could watch Grandfather sign on the big screen. I turned my chair but didn't need to watch because there was some guy at the end of the table interpreting for people who don't sign very well.

It was weird hearing this guy's voice attached to Grandfather's words. I know what Grandfather sounds like, and it wasn't like this guy. This guy had a high, whiny voice. I think that my grandfather's speech was written down and the guy was reading from the paper and not watching my grandfather because sometimes what he was saying and what my grandfather was signing were way off.

My grandfather is handsome, tall and pretty athletic-looking for an old guy. His hair is cut short to his head. It's mostly dark brown, but he has patches of gray. The gray doesn't make him look old, though. It makes him look smart.

My grandmother sat at the head table. Besides being the wife of the headmaster, she is also the school librarian. I watched my grandmother watch my grandfather as he signed.

Suddenly my grandmother turned from watching my grandfather and looked right at me. It was like she could feel my eyes on her. She smiled when she saw me. She held up her left hand, the pinkie and index finger sticking straight up, the middle two fingers folded down, and the thumb sticking out at a right angle. It's shorthand for "I love you." I held up my I-love-you hand back to her.

My grandmother's eyes twinkled.

My grandfather must have said something funny because the room was full of laughter. Not the *ha-ha* laughter you would hear from a group of hearing people, but loud nasal hoots and wails. The interpreter finally caught up with what my grandfather was saying, and then there were a few hearing people laughing.

Suddenly everyone's hands were in the air. Their fingers spread wide, palms facing out twisting back and forth, shimmering like leaves on a tree—deaf applause. There were a few people—hearing people, probably—who clapped the regular way at first. Then the sound of clapping stopped as everyone, hearing and deaf, put their hands in the air.

I really liked when they started showing the pictures. They started with pictures from seventy-five years ago. There weren't that many, which was good. They were in black and white and pretty boring. Then they got to when my parents went to school here. Those were cool. "Look," I signed, nudging Derek. "Your father!"

"Your father," he signed back. They were in football uniforms and covered with mud and dirt.

Mom was cute in her cheerleader outfit. In another picture she looked like a real jock in her lacrosse uniform.

As I looked around the room, I could see people glancing at our table. I could see what they were signing from three, four, even six tables away.

"Good family . . . strong Deaf."

"Strong Deaf," the other person agreed.

That's not "strong deaf" with a small *d*, but "strong Deaf" with a capital *D*.

Deaf with a small *d* just means you can't hear. But Deaf with a capital *D* means Deaf culture.

All the families in this room, at least the deaf families, knew that the Gilberts were a strong Deaf family. Perhaps the strongest Deaf family in the room.

marla —Much applause when finish. Grandfather good job. Pride fill gym. Pride fill me. Roommate meet cousin before leave. Not long talk. Roommate parent hurry away, because long drive home. I lucky. I stay Bradington all weekend.

Many people want talk with Gilbert family. Much talk. Much praise. Gilbert family last family in gym. Very dark. Parking lot empty.

Grandparent house near. Old house on lonely hill near school. Many tree make dark. See light bright from window far away.

Adult drive. Children walk.

Jade walk between cousin. Hold cousin hand. Jade demand cousin play. "Swing me!" Jade short. Cousin tall like swing in park. Walk two step, swing Jade high. Jade like baby. Need attention all time.

Because dark. Because baby play. No talk with cousin. Want ask Derek if like college roommate. Want ask about California spring vacation.

Cousin tired after much swing play. Put Jade down. Jade laugh. Sign, "Chase me."

Dillon chase Jade, pick up, throw on shoulder, run toward grandparent house. Good. Maybe arrive faster.

Baby away. Now time to talk like adult with Derek. Derek tell about first year Gallaudet. Class hard, but much time for play. No clean room inspection.

Love Bradington, but can't wait go Gallaudet. Gallaudet in Washington, D.C. Maybe visit White House. Maybe meet President.

Inside adult stay living room talk. Children run stair for big attic room.

Half room have bunk bed. Other half room have game, Ping-Pong table.

Ping-Pong table important. Grandfather Ping-Pong champion. Teach grandchildren play good. More Ping-Pong table in school game room. Gilbert students always best Ping-Pong player. Grandfather proud.

Want tournament now. Jade not want play. Tournament uneven.

Derek promise Jade five point because youngest. Plan: Jade, I play. Then Derek, Dillon play. Winner play winner.

I know before start, I win. Jade bad play.

Jade always open mouth when play. Look same fish.

"Sing when play?" I ask when win second point.

"No." Jade face show confuse.

"Not sing? Why mouth open? Try catch ball in mouth?"

Jade face red. Push mouth close. Angry face.

Mouth close not improve play.

I switch right hand.

I win game one point only.

"I better!" Jade tell Derek. "Lose only by one point!"

"Next time play, I use true hand." Move paddle from right hand to left hand.

Jade face angry. Stare. Throw paddle. Run from attic.

Want follow. Want scold. But cousin stop.

They want play now. Want me watch. Better this way. Jade gone. Jade bad sport.

JADE—The best part about going to Bradington for the weekend was staying at my grandparents' house, on a hill across the street from the school. I love the attic room on the third floor beneath the slanting rafters. It's a huge room with only one little window. I left the window open last night. The house is old and has lots of big trees around it, filled with birds. Birdsong filled the room before it was even light out.

I woke to the smell of cocoa. Not the instant stuff that comes out of packet. Grandmother always makes real cocoa with cream and sugar and lots of dark cocoa. It's thick and delicious.

"Morning Girl! Happy because have granddaughter like me—morning girl," Grandmother signed as I came into the kitchen.

This was the very best part of staying at my grandparents' house, getting alone time with my grandmother. Everyone in the family is a late sleeper. Everyone but me and Grandmother. Mornings are our special time together.

Grandmother got her coffee and nodded toward the back porch. We sat on the porch swing. She wrapped a soft afghan around me and I snuggled into her side.

The morning air was cool, fresh, moist, and exhilarating. Birds flitted in the bushes.

For as long as I can remember, my grandmother has had short hair. Very, very short hair. Cut close to her head like a man's haircut, but no one would confuse my grandmother for a man. She is beautiful. Even at six in the morning, she is always dressed for the day and looks elegant.

I sipped at the cocoa. Mmmm. Warm and sweet.

There was no need to say anything, just snuggle.

When the cocoa and the coffee were gone, Grandmother tapped me on my knee. "Time for bake breakfast roll. Help?"

I nodded.

We mixed the ingredients in a giant pottery bowl. I liked the way the dough felt as we kneaded it. We placed it on a wooden breadboard and covered it with a clean dishtowel.

Once the dough was rising I put the brown sugar, nuts, and butter in the bottom of the pan. We rolled out the dough and cut it into long strips, then rolled it up and put the soft warm circles in the pan. We stuck the pan in the oven. Five minutes later, the smell wafted throughout the house. Soon everyone—even Marla, who claims she has to sleep till noon every day because her stupid teen magazine said so—came stumbling down the stairs.

The sticky buns made it hard to sign, so everyone ate without talking. There was lots of finger-licking, slurping, and lip-smacking going on that morning.

I noticed that Derek and Dillon both had coffee with their sticky buns. Grandmother had made enough cocoa for me to have seconds and for Marla to have a mug or two, but when Marla saw Derek and Dillon having coffee, she decided to have a cup. She thinks she's so grown up. At her first sip she made a loud groaning sound. No one else in the room noticed, so I nudged Dillon, who was sitting next to me, and pointed in Marla's direction.

He didn't have to hear the groan—the look on her face said it all. *Yuck!*

"Need cream, sugar maybe," Dillon signed, pushing the sugar bowl toward her.

Marla pretended she liked the coffee just as it was. "No, want black same you," she signed.

I nudged Dillon and laughed. He smiled and sipped his coffee.

When Dillon looked away, Marla glared at me. Her cheeks were bright red. Served her right for making fun of me at Ping-Pong.

Once the dishes were put in the sink and the sticky fingers were washed, signing resumed. I pulled on Dillon's arm and asked him to come play a game with me. He patted my head and kept on signing. He and Derek were telling my parents and grandparents about something that happened at school. Something about the president.

"President U.S.?" I asked.

Derek signed, "No, college." He glanced at me for only an instant before his eyes went back to what Dillon was saying.

I went back upstairs and played a game of solitaire.

marla—Weekend fun. Play many game. Play card, Qwirkle, Blokus, Ping-Pong. When play Ping-Pong, Jade disappear. Like magic. Good time ask cousin question concern Gallaudet. Learn big problem because new president.

Cousin say problem same problem when parent Gallaudet student long ago. Board hire hearing president. Insult! How hearing lead Deaf? Now same problem.

When drive home, tap Mother seat.

"Both you, Father go student protest?"

Mother nod. Face very serious. "Make many sign. Stay out in rain, cold. No comfort for many day. But important."

"Protest success?"

"Yes. Hearing president quit. Hire deaf."

"Now problem again? Hearing president?"

"Not same problem. Not hearing, but not born deaf."

"Start deaf when adult?"

"No. Maybe four, maybe five year old. But learn speech, not sign language. Think hearing way best. Not true Deaf. No learn sign language until after twenty."

"After twenty year old?"

Mother nod. Eye show disbelief.

"Board dishonest. Because hire summer think avoid protest. Think Deaf not notice."

"Cousin think if not change, cancel summer vacation. Go Gallaudet. Protest."

"Good plan. But hope protest not necessary. Hope board smarter now. Jade awake? Need ask about shoe. Baseball next week. Have right shoe? Shoe fit?"

I touch Jade arm. Eye open.

"Mother need know. Shoe fit good? Practice start Tuesday."

"No! Practice is on Wednesday."

"No! Confuse. Practice start Tuesday."

Jade point finger my face. "Your team practice on Tuesday." Jade put hand on chest. "*My* team practice on Wednesday."

Jade act like older sister. Act more important. "Dumb. Play same team," I sign.

Jade face show confuse. "What? No. You're in senior league. I'm junior league."

"Confuse. Wrong."

"Not wrong!"

"Yes! Wrong!"

"I'm not old enough to play in the senior league. You have to be thirteen. I'm only twelve."

"You not give attention. Father tell you before summer vacation. No attention. That why confuse now."

"What are you talking about?"

Mother turn, tap knee. "What for? What wrong?"

"Jade problem. Always problem."

Mother wave hand for attention. "Need shoe?"

Put hand up. Give up.

Jade wave hand for attention. "Not understand! Explain!"

"Ask Mother. Not include me."

JADE—Marla pulled a pillow forward from the back. She pounded her fist into it several times to punch it into the right shape. She placed it in the crook between her shoulder and neck and leaned up against the SUV door.

I stuck my arm out and waved my hand to get her attention. When that didn't work, I pounded my hand on the seat next to her. "How can I be in the senior league?" I asked again when she looked back at me. "I'm not old enough."

"Talk parent," she signed again before shutting her eyes.

"Wait! Tell me! I don't understand," I signed, but she had already closed her eyes, shutting me out again.

I pounded the seat next to her until the vibrations forced her eyes to pop open.

Marla gave me a look of disgust before she waved a hand to get Mom's attention.

The two exchanged a flurry of signs.

I've signed since I was an infant, but there are times when I can't keep up with conversations between Mom and Marla. I could tell by their facial expressions that they were disgusted, probably with me.

"Not include me," Marla repeated before repositioning the pillow against the SUV door and shutting her eyes again.

"What problem?" Mom asked as she struggled to turn around to talk to me.

"Marla said both same team. How possible?" I asked.

Mom took in a big breath and snorted it out loudly like a bull about to charge. "Father make plan go same team, same time, more ease."

"But my friends," I signed back.

My father glanced over at my mother and signed, "What for?" That's the way deaf people ask *Why?* or *What's going on?* He couldn't see any of the conversation in the back seat.

I leaned toward the center so I could see what my mom signed in response.

"Jade," she signed to Dad. "Difficult. Always difficult."

He flipped on the turn signal. The loud blinking seemed to fill the inside of the SUV. He was going to pull over on the side of the interstate to talk to me about this. I sort of panicked. I'd seen too many episodes of *Cops* with cars getting hit on the side of the highway. But then I saw the exit sign for the rest area, and I breathed a sigh of relief.

Mom signed something to Dad that I couldn't see. The instant the SUV rolled to a stop, she and Marla jumped out of the SUV and headed to the restroom, signing as they went. Their backs were to me, so I wasn't sure what they were saying. They never looked back.

Dad unhooked his seatbelt and turned so he was facing me. "What problem?" Dad asked.

"Marla and I same team?"

"Yes," Dad said, looking surprised. "You important. You only twelve-year-old move up!"

My mouth fell open. I didn't know what to say. I didn't know what to sign. A whimpering sound came out of my mouth. It was a helpless sound. Dad did not hear. He could not hear. He took my open mouth as surprise, not despair.

"Go bathroom now. Not stop again before home." He opened the door, stepped outside the SUV, and motioned for me to get out as well.

I got out and shut the door behind me. Dad hit the remote to lock the doors. The locks clamped shut with a loud click. The horn honked. I jumped.

Dad walked around the car and gave me a hug. When he pulled back, I signed, "But my friends . . ."

"Make new friends."

"But all older. All Marla friends."

Dad gave me another thumbs-up gesture and ruffled my hair.

"Fun. Think you baby sister. Think cute. Think you M-A-S-C-O-T," he fingerspelled.

This was going to be a nightmare.

marla—Mother go store for buy Jade shoe. I not need new shoe, stay home. Start empty school box. Clean room for Mother pride.

Find last year softball picture. This third team. Team player change, but some stay same.

Have three friend. One friend name Gretel. Same name girl with brother Hansel from fairy story. Like tease about brother.

Have no brother. Gretel short, fat, good pitcher, nice.

Two friend twin. Twin name: Juniper, Willow. Name like tree. Girl tall like tree. First learn name, think joke. But more know, more like. Good name. Good match. Twin good sport player. Very pretty. Dark hair, dark eyes. Same me. People think three together triplet, not twin plus friend. Tree name special same twin special.

At Christmas vacation I visit. Snow much. Good sled hill near twin house. Much time. Much fun. Twin send valentine card. Twin send birthday present. Text sometime. Send funny card other time. Roommate jealous because many letter. At Easter vacation we go pizza.

Twin fingerspell good. Reason: practice together. Sign not good like fingerspell, but learn fast.

Work many hour. Finish. All school box empty. Finish room clean.

Text twins. Juniper answer first. Willow answer soon. Much excite. Tomorrow see first time after long not see.

Must tell twin problem. Sister Jade same team this year. Not happy. Jade very young. Same baby. Maybe big problem.

Willow mistake, think I worry for Jade.

Twin promise to help make Jade happy.

Tell twin some people like difficult. Impossible make happy.

Not tell twin, no worry for Jade. Worry for team!

JADE—"If Marla tells me to stop pouting one more time, I'm going to lose it."

Tana didn't say anything, she just let me talk. It was nice having someone listen to me.

"Ever since we returned from Bradington, every time she sees me she tells me I look like a sad dog or an unhappy rat or some stupid thing."

We were sitting on the swings at the park, just rocking back and forth slightly. The chains squeaked and groaned more loudly than if we were swinging high.

"Marla is only twenty months older than I am, but you'd think she's twenty *years* older the way she bosses me around. She's always telling me what to do, or correcting me. She acts more like my mother than my sister. Yesterday I was signing 'lemon' and she got all bent out of shape. She told me I used the wrong sign. That she thought I'd said 'lunch' and what I said made no sense."

"What's the sign for 'lemon'?"

I put an *L* hand on my chin near the corner of my mouth.

"What's the sign for 'lunch'?"

I moved my *L* hand an inch or so lower, closer to the center of my chin. "I think she could have figured out what I was saying by the context. *Lemon* pie is my favorite, not lunch pie! If she's so grown up and smart, you'd think she could figure that out."

I pushed off so my swing went side to side instead of back and forth. I moved away from Tana and then toward her, bumping her slightly. The chains clinked together above our heads.

"She acts like she's so grown up and nothing I ever do measures up to her adult standards. She better not boss me around at softball."

Neither of us said anything for what seemed like a whole minute.

"I wish you were going to be there."

Tana didn't say anything but tapped her foot against mine.

"When Mom took me shopping for shoes, I tried to get her to explain to me how I ended up being in the senior league when I wasn't even a starter in the junior league last year. I don't think she understood what I was asking. She just kept signing, 'Decision finish. No change.'"

"I talked to my dad about it," Tana said slowly as she moved away from me and then toward me.

"Yeah?"

"He called the guy in charge of organizing the league. They're friends from work. He called to see if he could find out anything from him."

"And?"

"Well . . . your dad emailed this organizer guy and asked him to get you on the same team. I guess they emailed each other back and forth for a while, and finally the organizer guy thought maybe you needed to be on the same team so you could interpret for Marla."

"What?"

"Well, Dad said that was the excuse he used for bumping you up."

"That's not it at all! Dad just didn't like driving to two different practices and having us play at two different times!"

"And after all the time we spent practicing running wind sprints and fielding grounders."

"Yeah! I was sure I was going to make first string this year.

Fat chance, now that I'll be the youngest member of the team."

Tana reached across and put her hand on my knee. "Don't say that! You worked hard! You really improved."

I put my arms around Tana and the chains clinked together loudly.

"I'm really going to miss you," Tana whispered in my ear.

I couldn't say anything because there was a big frog in my throat. Tears squeezed from my eyes and I hugged Tana tighter. I nodded instead.

marla—Feeling like ant army march under hand. Whole arm feel buzz from SUV side. Like attack from bee.

Jade sit front same Father. Father make music loud. All SUV shake.

Father hand on radio top. See Father sign, "How music sound? Good? Bad? Like song?"

"Like song!" Jade sign back. "Favorite. Name: 'I'm No Hero.'"

Father hit radio top like hit drum.

Jade shut eye, sing word into imagine microphone. Good! No room for elephant dance.

Father try make Jade happy. Jade want quit. Not play softball because not with friend Tana. "See Tana all time. What problem?" I ask Father. Father not see that Jade not want happy. Jade like problem. Jade like misery.

Father demand promise to help Jade feel special.

"Not my idea have Jade same team. Not my problem. Jade problem. Father problem."

Father say older sister responsible one.

Calendar hide under bed say sixty-two day before return Bradington.

JADE—When we got to the practice field, I felt like I'd arrived at the land of the giants.

Marla already knew some of the girls. They'd been on her team last year. Her twin friends came running over right away. They're named for trees, Willow and Juniper. Maybe everyone on the team is named for trees. They're all tall as trees.

Willow and Juniper had big smiles on their faces. "Hi!" they said in unison like they were part of a Doublemint commercial. "Glad you're here. Marla's told us so much about you."

I gave them a funny look. Like I believe that Marla told them much about me. Obviously they didn't understand what she said. Marla never has anything nice to say to me or about me.

I didn't say anything, just pushed my lips together. Mom tells me all the time, "If you don't have anything nice to say, don't say anything at all." Somehow that rule doesn't apply to Marla.

Coach Smuckers was the same coach Marla had last year. He was wearing shorts and a ball cap. "Okay, girls! Over here!" he called out as he waved to us.

I made sure I was standing on the other side of the group, away from Marla, the twins, and Marla's other friend, Gretel. Coach Smuckers gave us a rah-rah speech about how he was looking forward to a great year and told us he'd give us the schedule and hand out uniforms at the end of practice.

He clapped his hands at the end of the speech and said, "Okay! Let's start by running laps around the field. When I call out your name, come over and we'll talk about what position you're interested in playing. Other than that . . . keep running until I tell you to stop. I'm going alphabetically, so Benes and Carlton, don't start. Just stay here."

Everyone except those two girls took off running counter-clockwise around the field. I was in the middle of the pack at first, but by the time we had turned in toward center field I was lagging far behind everyone else. Okay, so I'm not the world's fastest runner, but they all had such long legs. I had to run twice as fast to cover the same distance.

I was starting to worry that the entire group would lap me. Luckily, by the time I made it back around home plate, Coach Smuckers called out "Gilbert! Jade!" and I trotted over to him.

When he took his eyes off the clipboard and looked at me for the first time, I could tell he was surprised by how short I was. "You are only two years younger than Marla?" he asked.

I nodded.

His eyebrows scrunched together, and he looked me up and down like he didn't believe me. "What year were you born?"

When I told him, his eyes looked upward as he calculated. Then, convinced at last, he switched back into coach mode. "Okay! What position do you like to play, Jade?"

"First base."

"First base! Hmm." He nodded, seemingly impressed with my choice, and he wrote something on the clipboard.

I wanted to tell him that I'd been working for weeks with my stretch, with getting in front of the ball and practicing catching.

But I stood there like my feet were permanently planted in the infield dirt and my lips were temporarily glued shut.

"Got a lot of returning players this year, and our infield is pretty well set. How 'bout we try you in right field first and work up to the infield?"

I nodded to let him know I heard what he said. No one ever hits to right field. And who's kidding who—I'm going to be sitting on the bench most of the season.

"Gilbert! Marla!" he called out. "Oh, guess you can stay right here."

"I'm Jade."

"Yeah, but you'll probably want to interpret for your sister."

"I probably don't," I said under my breath as Coach Smuckers looked around for my sister. When he saw her, he waved her over.

I wish I had enough guts to turn around and walk away, but the chicken in me only allowed me to shuffle back a couple of steps.

"Po-Zi-Shun," Coach Smuckers said loudly and slowly with exaggerated lip movement, as if each syllable was a different word. Then he pointed to Marla and put his hands up in a questioning gesture.

Marla didn't look in my direction. She held up three fingers—thumb, index, and middle finger. Sign language for the number three.

Coach Smuckers smiled, nodded, and wrote it down.

Marla played third base last year. See! Coach Smuckers didn't need me at all. I turned and walked back to the dugout and sat by myself on the bench. Marla caught up to her group of friends and kept running. No one seemed to notice or care that I wasn't running.

It didn't take long for Coach Smuckers to finish. Then he called us all over for another pep talk. He told us this year we were going to work hard on fielding. "I want you each to learn to get in front of the ball and stop it. I want each one of you to think of yourself as a wall that no ball can get past."

Out of the corner of my eye I could see Willow (or was it Juniper?) fingerspelling W-A-L-L to Marla.

"Next practice, my assistant coach, Coach Williams, will be here to work with you on your hitting. Make sure you bring your gloves. Now pick up your schedules and see Mrs. Smuckers about your uniform before you leave."

Everyone ran over to get in line for Mrs. Smuckers.

I waited until no one was left, then walked over. Mrs. Smuckers was packing up her things and getting ready to leave.

"Jade Gilbert," I said.

"Oh!" she said, looking at her clipboard. "I guess I do have one more name on the list. I didn't realize you were a player. I thought maybe you were someone's little sister here to watch."

Great.

"My goodness," she said. "You're much smaller than the other girls. I only ordered two smalls this year and I've already handed them out. All I have left is an extra-large, and that won't do. I'll exchange it for a small. It might take a couple of weeks, but we'll get you that uniform."

"Okay," I said and turned to walk away. "Doesn't really matter," I muttered to myself. "I'm going to be sitting on the bench."

"Where uniform?" Dad asked when he came to pick us up.

"No order uniform for M-A-S-C-O-T," I signed and went to the SUV.

Marla was already in the front seat. She and Dad signed about practice all the way home.

One practice down, twenty-nine practices and twelve games to go. It was going to be a long summer.

marla—Last night twin text news. Hear reason from coach why Jade on team. Reason: Interpret.

Not true! I text back. *No interpret before. Why now?*

Twin not answer. Text other news.

After text finish, anger grow. I not need interpret from Jade. Independent always.

Next practice, two coach. One Coach Smuckers. Other Coach Williams. Coach S teach catch, field. Coach W teach hit ball. Coach W new.

Coach W call each girl separate. But Jade, me together.

Other player practice. Improve catch, field. I stand. Watch Jade practice hit ball. Not good plan. Waste practice time.

Coach W throw slow to Jade. Jade swing. Miss. Coach W talk. Jade nod. Throw again. Miss again. Jade face angry. No patient. Want easy. Not want work.

Throw third time. Miss. Jade stomp foot. Bad sport.

I wave hand for attention. "Maybe try open mouth same Ping-Pong."

"Shut up!"

"Rude!" I sign back.

"*You* rude. You're mean to me."

"You bug. Annoy, same bug."

Jade throw bat to ground. Walk away. Yell back and forth with coach.

Rude. Jade speech only, not sign.

Coach speak. Jade throw hard bat hat.

Time seem long. Not knowing next action.

Coach W wave hand, point hard bat hat, point bat. Pick up. Put on. I stand, ready for throw.

Coach W not throw, but shake head.

Say word, point mouth, open mouth big O—much exaggerate.

Not understand.

Coach W show fist together. That sign? Or teach hand on bat? Look coach hand. Look my hand. Look same.

Coach get wipe-off clipboard. Write big letter. *CHOKE.*

Choke? Put hand on throat. Not choke. Try voice. "Fine," I say. Speech teacher, Mr. Hendley, say my speech good. Coach W face show confuse. Not understand.

He write more on board. *Choke up on bat.*

I eat bat? I choke?

Juniper see problem communication, come help.

She not know signs for words and must fingerspell all sentence. "Means move hands up on bat."

Oh! Why not write, *Move hands up on bat*?

Speech teacher say name for phrase like "choke up on bat" is *idiom*. Hearing use many idiom. Make confuse.

"Where is Jade? She can interpret better than I can," Juniper half signed and half fingerspelled.

"Tell coach, not need Jade for interpret. Write. Not use idiom." Because Juniper not know sign for "interpret," I fingerspell word, then show sign. No sign for "idiom," must fingerspell again. Make communicate much time.

Coach W throw many ball. I hit many ball. Miss maybe two. Maybe three. One hit go far.

Coach W eye grow big. Face show surprise, impress.

Look, see Jade. Jade practice fielding. Run for low ball. Stop ball. Jade quick.

Finish. Go back to catch, field practice. See Coach W talk to Jade. Arm on shoulder. Talk long. Jade practice hit. Mouth no open, but hit. Not far. But hit four, six, maybe eight hit.

Much thirst when practice finish. Water good.

Before Father arrive, twin talk. Gretel talk.

"Sister good for only twelve."

"Very short."

"Cute!"

"Think how much better she would be if she were taller," Willow say.

Not think before that if taller maybe better player.

"Very good at ground ball," Gretel say. Gretel know only sign for "good" and "ball." She fingerspell all other word.

"Better than me when I was twelve," Willow, Juniper sign same time. Laugh.

"Do all time . . ."

"Say same thing . . ."

"Same time."

Twin say have good idea. Maybe Gilbert sister stay night with twin. I say no. "Jade afraid sleep away from home. Jade baby."

"Maybe she feel better with her big sister," Willow sign.

I say I text later. But later I text that Jade say no.

True answer: I not ask.

Jade have friend Tana. Jade sad no time with Tana. Not take more time from other friend. Willow, Juniper *my* friend.

JADE—At every practice, Coach Williams and Coach Smuckers promised me they'd have my uniform before the first game. I'd shrug. I thought that maybe they should just get a mascot uniform for me. Maybe they should put INTERPRETER on the back, which was the only reason the coaches thought I was there anyway.

If I were in the junior league on the same team with Tana, I'd probably be playing first base. But as our practice started today, I could only imagine that I was playing first base. I ran to first base and held out my glove, stretched my leg behind me, and pretended to catch a high throw, making sure my toe stayed on the base. I found the imaginary ball in my glove and threw it to third base. Then I pretended to throw it hard in a straight line to the catcher, who tagged the player before she could step on the plate. Out number three. I jumped up. Cheering not just for me, but a team I was part of.

"Looks like you got them out," a voice said from behind.

I jumped and turned around to see who had been watching me. It was Gretel. She was the next-shortest player on the team. Still lots taller than me, but at least I wasn't looking at her belly button.

"Hey, you ever thought of being a catcher?"

"Catcher?"

"Yeah! I've been watching you. You're really good about getting in front of the ball. The ball never gets by you, and that's great for a pitcher. I mean, pitchers like catchers who never let their pitch get by them."

I pushed my lips together. I'd never thought of being a catcher before. I didn't say anything to Gretel, but I was sort of worried about getting hit. Hit by the ball. Hit by the bat. Hit by a giant running from third to home plate.

"Hey, Coach! Tezcan didn't show up today. Can I use Jade here as catcher?"

Coach Smuckers stared at Gretel, then at me, then shrugged and said, "Why not." I was a nobody on his team anyway.

As Gretel pitched to me, she sort of chanted in a slow, steady rhythm, "Pitchers are cool. Catchers rule." She kept saying that over and over again until I found that I was saying it too. It was sort of mesmerizing.

We have two pitchers on the team and two players that play other positions and sometimes pitch. Stroh usually catches, and Tezcan is the backup catcher. Tezcan has already missed two out of six practices.

"From now on, you're my practice catcher," Gretel says. "Okay?"

"Sure."

For the first time I felt like I had a place on the team. For the first time I had a smile on my face as I climbed in the back of the SUV. Marla was already in the front seat with Dad. They were exchanging a flurry of signs. Dad felt the door close and glanced back to make sure I was in the car before he took off and headed home. As he drove, he continued to sign to Marla. His face looked serious.

When we got home I saw Mom's car in the driveway. Mom was home early. That's when I knew something was up.

Marla and Dad took the front steps two at a time and disappeared inside.

When I came through the front door, Mom was just on her way up the stairs with a basket of laundry. Moments later she came clomping back downstairs with a packed suitcase and placed it by the door. She dashed to the dining room table, passing within inches of me, but I swear she didn't even know I was there. She wrote something on a list. She was so focused on getting ready to leave that I didn't dare ask her any questions.

Marla and Dad came from the kitchen still signing continuously. Dad went upstairs.

"What?" I ask Marla.

"Gallaudet problem. Protest. Parents leave."

"Both?"

"Yes. Yes, all go. Parents, Aunt Kelly, Uncle Andrew, cousins, grandparents."

"Leave? For how long?"

"What necessary."

"Two days? One week? A month?"

Marla held up her hands to indicate she had no idea.

When Dad came down the stairs with another suitcase, I asked, "Marla and I stay alone?"

"No, no. Grandmother H coming now. Call hour past. Soon here."

I smiled. Good. For a minute there, I thought they'd leave me here alone with Marla. She would morph into super-bossy mode in an instant.

Marla also saw what Dad signed. "Grandmother H? No! No need babysitter. Old enough to stay home alone."

"Need drive to softball practice, game. You no drive."

That response stopped Marla in her tracks. I could see her eyes moving side to side. She was thinking. She stopped Dad before he went back upstairs. She pulled on his shirt sleeve and he turned around. "I go Gallaudet."

Dad looked surprised. "No. Have softball."

"My future more important than softball. I strong Deaf. I future Gallaudet student."

Mom came down the stairs at this moment with her cosmetic bag. She stopped on the fourth step, the first time she had stopped moving since I'd walked in the door. "What for?" she asked, sensing the question in the air.

"Marla want come," Dad answered.

"No," Mom signed. She continued down the stairs.

"I want fight for strong Deaf," Marla signed. "Fight for good education. *My* education. Gallaudet my future. Important go. Important fight for future."

Those words touched Mom. I could see it in her eyes. Her lips were firmly pressed together, but her jaw moved in tiny circles as she thought about what Marla had said.

"Father, I talk private."

My parents went into the living room and huddled together with their backs to the foyer. Marla sat on the floor in the foyer, leaning against the living room wall. I couldn't resist peering around the corner to see what they were talking about. Normally, Marla would have scolded me for spying on our parents, but this time she asked if I knew what they were saying.

I told Marla their backs were to me and I couldn't see anything . . . but I'd lied. I had seen a few signs. Signs that rooted my feet to the floor and made my knees shake a little. *Danger. Police. Arrest. Police record.*

Mom and Dad turned and I immediately sank to the floor next to Marla with my back against the wall like I hadn't been spying on them at all.

I even tried to look surprised when they came from the room and waved at Marla to join them. They didn't tell me I couldn't come in the room, but I stayed back by the door and watched the conversation from there.

"Sit," Mom told Marla, pointing to the couch.

Dad sat down next to her, and she turned to look at him.

"Very proud you want come—you want protest," Dad signed to Marla.

"Yes," Mom signed as she stood by my father, her face serious.

"But fight for future for adult. For parent. Not girl, fourteen."

"You need stay here. Play softball. Support home."

"Be strong Deaf here."

Marla did not argue. She didn't have time. Mom and Dad dropped a kiss on Marla's head, kissed me as they walked by, and grabbed the bags waiting for them next to the front door. Marla and I followed them outside to the SUV.

"Grandmother H here soon. Be good," Mom signed through the window after she closed the SUV door.

Each showed us their I-love-you hands as they backed out of the driveway. Marla and I stood side by side in the drive and showed our I-love-you hands back to them.

marla—Grandmother H not here one hour. Not here two hour.

Jade worry, want phone. I not worry. I true understand. Grandmother H bad plan. Late many time.

Not remember Grandfather H. Only remember picture of Grandfather H when hold baby me.

Grandfather H maybe die because too much annoy. Grandmother H mouth open always. When young, draw picture Grandmother H with mouth always open. Grandmother H talk all time. Never sign. Mouth open too much. Surprise bug not live in mouth.

When young, idea start that *H* mean *hearing*. Many year think *H* mean hearing grandparent before learn *H* mean last name Halpin, Mother last name before marry. Now Mother last name strong Deaf name Gilbert.

Always call grandparent at Bradington, Grandmother, Grandfather. Never say Grandmother Gilbert or Grandmother G or Grandmother D for Deaf. Feel that Bradington grandparents true grandparents. Feel that Grandmother H not true grandparent.

Three hours after parent go, Grandmother H not here. Jade worry. Jade say she phone. Say Grandmother H no answer. Angry because tell Jade no phone. Make more worry. "Hungry now. Cook dinner."

Jade open pantry, get box Quaker Instant Oatmeal.

"Not funny."

But Jade no attention. Rude! Light flash in foyer mean some-one here.

Jade run. Need look first before door open. Use voice for Jade attention. Wave for Jade attention. But Jade no attention. Jade run. No look, but open door.

Maybe bad person! Maybe thief!

Not thief. Grandmother H.

Jade hug Grandmother H. Big hug. Jade talk. Grandmother H talk. Rude! Not sign. I stand foyer, wait. Not notice me. Maybe Grandmother H believe I not true granddaughter because not hearing.

Jade think all better because Grandmother H here. Wrong!

Before parents leave, Father say I strong Deaf. Support home.

Grandmother H think she house boss. Wrong!

This Deaf house. Hearing not boss Deaf house, same as hearing not boss Deaf university.

JADE—I couldn't remember exactly when Mom and Dad left. It was after softball practice and before dinnertime. I remember thinking Mom was home early, so it was before five, but sometime after four. Dad said Grammy would be here in about an hour.

I looked at the clock. It was after eight.

Even if I had been way off about when they left, Grammy

should have gotten to our house long before that. What if something happened to her? What if she was in a car accident?

As soon as Mom and Dad left, Marla had started texting. I figured she was texting Tabitha and Jasmine, but it went on for the next two hours straight. For all I knew, she was texting everyone in her class at Bradington. Her thumbs were moving back and forth so fast that I thought they might fly off.

"Grandmother H not here. Worry," I signed.

Marla looked up at me, but her thumbs kept moving on the keyboard. She couldn't say anything, as her hands were busy, but her face said it all. *Stop being so stupid! What a baby!*

I went to my room to get my cellphone.

Marla followed me, texting as she walked.

She shook her head when I picked up my cellphone. She stopped long enough to sign, "Grandmother H bad drive. No phone! Stop worry. Grandmother H always late. Hungry now. Cook dinner."

As soon as she finished signing, her fingers went back to texting.

Dad works from home, but Mom runs the household, making sure everything is neat and organized. She also puts a work chart on the refrigerator to make sure we all pitch in to help. Dad and I like to cook, so long ago we decided my job was to help Dad cook dinner and clean up, and Marla's job was to do laundry and iron and fold clothes.

Not really fair when you think about it. Her job is once a week, and my job is every day.

Well, I wasn't hungry. So if she was hungry she could fix herself something to eat.

As soon as I heard the springs creak on Marla's bed, I got the cellphone out again and called Grammy. No answer.

When I told Marla she was mad. "Said not call. Not listen. Never listen older sister. I boss. Must do my word. Hungry now. Cook dinner."

Marla followed me downstairs to the kitchen. She was still texting away when I set the box of Quaker Instant Oatmeal in front of her. When she looked up and saw the box, that sick-cow sound came out of her again. I didn't want her to see my face. To see that I was laughing. I'm not that stupid. So I turned my back on her. She was calling out and stomping her foot on the floor to get my attention when the doorbell rang.

Oh, please let that be Grammy! I thought.

I ran to the door and unlocked it, and there she was! I threw my arms around her. Grammy had three plastic grocery bags hanging from each hand, so she couldn't hug me back, but I didn't care.

"Heaven's sakes!" she said. "Are you okay?"

Tears filled my eyes. "I was so worried about you! Dad said you'd be here hours ago."

"I was going to text them that it would take me an hour to pack, an hour to drive, and maybe an hour to do the grocery shopping. But I'd barely typed in *hour* when your father typed back *fine*."

I nodded. Grammy was really slow at text messaging. It would have taken her an hour to type all that.

"Well, not to worry, Jade. I'm here now. You okay?"

I nodded. I was okay now that she was here.

"Well, let me in. Let's get this door shut before the house fills up with bugs. They're awful this time of year."

I let go of Grammy and she shuffled forward with the grocery bags still dangling from her hands. I shut the door behind her.

"*Youuuuu ooooo-kaaaaaaay?*" Grammy said loudly to Marla.

Marla was standing on the first step of the stairs, leaning against the banister. Her arms were crossed in front of her, and she had a sour look on her face. She uncrossed her arms, touched her fingers to her ears, then threw her arms wide in a gesture that clearly meant, *I can't hear you. I'm deaf!*

Grammy put the grocery bags on the floor and struggled to free her right hand from the tangle of grocery bag handles so she could make an "okay" sign to Marla. But by the time her fingers were free, Marla had disappeared upstairs.

marla—Grandmother H arrive many hours late. Talk Jade. No sign. Understanding grow: Jade learn rude from Grandmother H.

Watch from upstairs window. Jade help Grandmother H carry suitcase. Carry more store bag. Jade talk, talk, talk while carry. Grandmother H talk, talk, talk.

Go room, but leave door open. Soon, hall light flash. Meaning: Dinner ready. I decide not eat dinner now. Wait. Eat later.

Hall light flash again.

I shut door.

See hall light flash again from under door.

Turn back and text-message friend from Bradington about Gallaudet president problem.

Room light flash. Turn around. Jade sign, "Come. Eat. Grandmother H bring chicken. Good."

Much hunger now. Stomach complain. "Not hungry now. Eat later." Lie.

Jade close door.

Look desk drawer. Find granola bar.

Hour later, Grandmother H come to room. Make "okay" sign. Nod. Look at phone.

Grandmother H wave hand for attention, hold arm open wide. Meaning: I want hug.

I no want hug. Look phone, text more. Maybe Grandmother H think not see.

Grandmother H have notebook. Take pen write: *Don't worry about your parents. They are fine. Must not worry. Must eat.*

I want tell Grandmother H I no worry parent. Parent fine. Parent smart. Parent strong Deaf. I not want eat because kitchen all hearing. All talk. No sign. Not include. My notebook on desk.

I wave hand meaning, no eat. But also meaning, no talk with you.

Grandmother H kiss forehead. Mouth words. Maybe first word "good." Not know other word.

Grandmother H put prayer hands against face and shut eyes. Understanding grow. Maybe mouth words are "good night."

Grandmother H show I-love-you hand and wait.

Hands text. I no show I-love-you hand back.

Grandmother H close mouth. Eyes look sad, disappoint. Grandmother H close door.

Anger grow. Wish with strong Deaf, not all hearing.

Remember story from Bradington classmate, name Shannon. Shannon start Bradington last year. Grade 1, 2, 3, 4, 5, 6, 7, 8—all grade, Shannon spend at hearing school. Shannon only deaf. Same in family, only deaf.

When come to Bradington Shannon say feel same Harry Potter. "Bradington like Hogwarts," Shannon tell us. "Before, I am wizard living in muggle world. Now I come Bradington, I discover I am wizard. I am special. I am magic. Summer vacation bad for Harry Potter. Bad same me. Misery. Hearing world not my family. Deaf world my family."

Understand story better. Now I live in world of muggle, not world of magic. Text Shannon my new understanding.

Go bathroom before sleep. Open door. Fall because box next to door. Pick up box. Dark. Difficult see.

Surprise when see. No belief! Box of Quaker Instant Oatmeal. Jade slay my good soul.

JADE—Usually I'm the first one up. Grammy doesn't get up as early as my deaf grandmother and she doesn't make hot cocoa from scratch. Still, it was nice coming downstairs to find Grammy in the kitchen, even if she was still wearing her robe.

Grammy had already made a pot of coffee and that coffee smell filled the kitchen.

"Can I make you bacon and eggs?" she asked.

I nodded.

"Should I make some for Marla?"

"Maybe later. Marla sleeps almost till noon every day."

Grammy shook her head. "She's turned into a real teenager, hasn't she?"

I nodded. "She has this idea that all teens sleep until noon. She even has this stupid magazine article that she shows to me every time I say something about how late she sleeps."

Grammy made a clucking sound with her tongue as she started to lay the bacon in the skillet. "She reminds me so much of your mother when your mother was her age."

"Really?" Marla looks like Dad's side of the family, so I guess I always thought that Marla was more like them.

"Your mother was always so . . ." Grammy paused and the bacon sizzled in the pan as I waited. "Difficult."

It seemed strange to hear that word describing Mom. Usually it's Mom signing "difficult" to describe me.

"When I walked into Marla's bedroom last night to see if she was okay, to see if she was hungry, to tell her not to worry about your parents, it was as if I'd stepped back in time. I could have sworn it was twenty years ago and I was in your mother's room and she was glaring at me. Glaring at me like a caged animal intent on escape. Summers were so long. Your mother hated being home. She never wanted to leave Bradington. I tried to make her favorite foods, to take her interesting places, but she always had that glum look on her face. She let me know every second of every day that she didn't want to be home for the summer. Summers were miserable for all of us."

I watched as Grammy turned the bacon with a pair of tongs. She turned them again and again until they were brown and crisp and the kitchen smelled of bacon.

"And what was all that noise about, around ten o'clock? Marla was out in the hall upset about something. I swear I heard something hit one of the doors upstairs."

"I think she tripped over something in the hall on her way to let Beezley out last night," I told Grammy. I tried not to laugh. It was the Quaker Instant Oatmeal box that I'd put in front of her door before I went to bed. I'd brought it downstairs this morning, one corner dented in.

Grammy got out another pan, sprayed it with Pam, and poured in the beaten-egg mixture.

"Have you heard from your parents? Did they email or text? I trust they got to your grandparents' place all right," Grammy said as she continuously turned the eggs in the pan.

"They're in D.C.," I said.

Grammy stopped and the room was strangely quiet. "I thought your father said it was an emergency. Something with your grandparents." She lifted the pan from the stove so the eggs wouldn't brown as she tried to remember. *"Emergency. Must meet parents, Deaf family. Need babysit girls,"* she said as if reading the text in front of her right now. She sounded as choppy and abrupt as my parents' texts often were. "I figured it was a family emergency. Something to do with your other grandparents."

"Well, they're all going. My grandparents. My aunt and uncle. Even my cousins. They went to D.C., something about protesting the new president of the university."

"Again? Your mother was involved in a protest when she was a student. They were all up in arms that the board of directors picked a hearing president. You would have thought they put Hitler in charge."

60

"I'll see what I can find out online after breakfast," I told Grammy.

The eggs were perfect and the bacon crisp. Grandmother Gilbert is a great baker, but Grammy is a great short-order cook. I hope she can teach me how to make my bacon crisp without getting any burnt spots.

After breakfast I pulled up an article online on Dad's computer about what was going on in Washington. The headline read: NEW GALLAUDET PRESIDENT NOT DEAF ENOUGH.

I called Grammy into Dad's office and had her read it. "Not deaf enough? I don't understand. I've never understood," Grammy said on the way back to the kitchen.

I sort of understood, but I didn't think I could explain it.

"It's like when Marla was born," Grammy said as she was loading the dishwasher.

I was glad she had her back to me and couldn't see my face. I was confused. I didn't see how this situation was connected with Marla's birth.

"Your grandfather and I were devastated," Grammy said. "Ninety percent of deaf couples have hearing children, you know, so we hoped, we prayed . . . but our darling, cute granddaughter was deaf." Grammy shut the dishwasher door and leaned against it, staring at the kitchen floor, her face sad. She shook her head and took a deep breath. "I begged your parents to get a cochlear implant for her."

"You did?"

"Yes! The doctors said she was a great candidate. She could be hearing, talking, not handicapped."

"I didn't know that."

"Oh, yes! I wish I had known more about them when your mother was little. By the time I learned about them, she was already in college, over eighteen. I told her I'd pay for it! But she just said, 'Why would I want to hear?' Can you imagine that? 'Why would I want to hear?'"

Grammy waved her yellow-plastic-kitchen-gloved hand as if to magically wipe away all those bad memories. Then she started babbling about some TV show she watched.

I tuned her out. My mind was still thinking about the cochlear implant. I'd heard talk about cochlear implants like they were evil mind-controlling devices. The sign for cochlear implant is just like the sign for vampire, only at the back of the head.

But beyond the argument over whether cochlear implants were evil or good was that odd thought: *What would it be like if Mom could hear?* I couldn't believe that that might have been possible and that Mom had chosen to stay deaf.

marla—Very hungry when wake up. Bacon smell. Good.

But in kitchen, no bacon. Kitchen empty. Instant oatmeal box on counter.

Tap on shoulder. Grandmother H mouth word. Speech only. No sign. First word maybe "good." Maybe say "good morning." But not good morning. Very, very hungry.

Grandmother H put hand to mouth, meaning: Eat. Yes.

Grandmother H point oatmeal. Nod head. Eye ask, "Want?" Shake head no.

Grandmother H write in notebook: *Jade said you might want oatmeal for breakfast.*

Take notebook from Grandmother H, write: *Jade lie! Hate oatmeal! Want bacon and eggs!*

Grandmother H nod, but face show disgust. Think me mean, rude. Grandmother H not understand. Jade problem.

Time slow before softball practice.

Read Internet news about Gallaudet. All time read computer. All time text friend. No leave office but for Beezley outside.

Grandmother H drive car. Jade sit front, point way. Wrong way two time. Not ask me. I know way. Late to practice. Grandmother H always late. Not good plan.

Practice start many minute before. Run, meet team.

Twin ask, "Who car? Where father?"

No time describe. Face show all. Serious problem.

After practice, try communicate.

Grandmother H wave hand. I turn back. No attention.

Jade run tap shoulder. "Grandmother H want come now. Home now."

"Wait! Late because you bad way. No ask me. I know way. No attention Deaf."

Jade face angry, mean.

"Go Grandmother H," I sign.

Jade run away.

Twin face serious. No understanding sign with Jade. Too fast for understand.

"What wrong?" Juniper ask.

Willow eye big. "Parents okay?'

"Who?" Juniper ask, point to Grandmother H.

"Other grandmother. Grandmother H-E-A-R-I-N-G," I fingerspell for twin.

"You have a grandmother that can hear?"

Annoy. Not want talk grandmother. Want talk Gallaudet problem.

Twin not look at me, look behind me.

Turn. Disappoint. Grandmother H, Jade come.

Grandmother H talk. Mouth open. Mouth close. Talk fast. Smile. Laugh.

Twin not talk me. Listen Jade. Listen Grandmother H. Nod head.

Twin sign now. "Understand now. Parents in D.C."

Twin wrong. Twin not understand. This not fun visit Gallaudet. This protest. This strong Deaf struggle! No smile. No laugh. No simple understand.

Communication broke. No goodbye. Go car. Wait.

Grandmother H, Jade talk, talk, talk.

Shut eye. Wait in car.

Pizza for dinner. Stay room all night.

Twin text. Ask problem.

Text back website for Gallaudet information on protest. Maybe true understand after read. No other answer.

Next day, first game.

Jade wake me. Very early. "Need clothes wash. Need clean pants for game today."

"Ask Grandmother H."

"No! Your job!"

"Grandmother H do your job, cook. Grandmother H do my job, wash clothes. Go away. Close door."

Clothes folded in kitchen. Grandmother H fold wrong. Must fold again. Not one thing right!

Grandmother H come kitchen. Smile big. Mouth words. Grandmother H open, close mouth. Speech only. No sign. No respect.

I point ear. Pull hand out empty.

Grandmother H write notebook: *Don't worry. Your parents are fine.*

I write notebook: *Not worry parents. Sad for mother because she have bad mother. Not respect Deaf. Not sign. Speech only.*

Not wait for Grandmother H answer. Go room.

Not see Grandmother H again. Wait all afternoon for game time.

Go car. Wait car. Watch time. Honk horn. Must hurry no late again.

JADE—"Come on, Samantha, you can do it," Gretel called out and clapped her hands. Then she leaned over and whispered to me, "I'm not sure if she has anything left. If she can just hang on . . ."

Samantha threw a pitch that looked too low to me, but the batter swung at it.

Gretel was on her feet cheering so loud that I didn't hear the ump call out, "Strike two."

"Full count now, Samantha! One more! One more. You can do it!" Gretel leaned into my shoulder and patted my knee. "Batter. Batter, batter, swwwwing batter," she chanted.

The pitch went over the plate. The batter went down swinging. Our first game was over. We had won!

Gretel jumped from the bench and ran out to the pitcher's mound to join the rest of the team in one jumping, cheering mass, high fives all around. Marla was beaming! It was the first time I'd seen her smile since our parents left, but then, she had a lot to smile about.

The major reason our team was jumping up and down on the mound was that Marla had played a great game. She got three hits, batted in two runs, and scored two runs. And that was just on offense. Defensively, she was a terror. She stopped every ball that came close to her. Once, she dove for a ball hit her way. It was a great catch. I doubted that anyone else on the team could have snagged it. It would have been a two-base hit with anyone but Marla at third base.

The girls stopped jumping up and down on the pitcher's mound long enough for a group hug. Everyone except me. I didn't feel like I had much to do with the win, so I stayed on the bench. I'd spent the entire game there.

I would be sitting on the bench for the rest of the season. Maybe in games that were blowouts, they'd allow me to stand in right field.

I turned around and looked at Grammy, who was sitting in the stands by herself. She gave me a big thumbs-up and applauded. Poor Grammy! She just doesn't quite know what to do or say to Marla.

A couple of hours before the game, she showed me the note Marla had written. "I've never been good at signing," she told me. "And I don't see you guys that much. If you don't use it, you lose it."

I spent the rest of the afternoon until we left for the game teaching her a few phrases. One was "Good game." As I looked at Grammy now, she signed "good" very slowly and then had to think about how to sign "game," which she finally remembered and came close to signing correctly. She was almost as slow at signing as she was at texting.

I gave her a thumbs-up and was happy she didn't have to use the other phrase I taught her, which was twice as long: "Better luck next time."

It was a huge relief that the game had been at our home field. If Grammy had had to drive us to a different field and had gotten lost again, Marla would have freaked.

Marla was sitting in Grammy's car an hour before the game was going to start. We didn't even know she was there until she started beeping the horn. Grammy almost had a heart attack.

Now Gretel turned and motioned for me to come to the mound, but the group was starting to break up. She jogged back over to the bench, where she'd sat next to me the whole game.

"Wow! What a great game!" she said.

"Yeah. Not that I had anything to do with it."

"What do you mean? You helped me warm up." Gretel put her arm around my shoulder and pulled me close.

"Yeah, but you didn't pitch."

"But I might have needed to pitch. Being here, being ready to go in—that's important. Think what a psychological disadvantage it would be if our team on the field looked at the bench and didn't see anyone to back them up."

I looked at her like she was crazy.

"Come on. Lighten up. So you didn't play in the first game. That doesn't mean you're going to sit on the bench all year."

I didn't say anything, but she could tell from my eyes that that was exactly what I thought.

"I'll bet you that not only will you play, but you'll make a game-winning play."

"Really?"

"Yup."

"We'll see."

"No, *you'll* see!"

marla —Grandmother H sign "good" and then "game." Awkward. Slow. But understand. I nod.

When left for softball, no news from parents for long time. Not know how long protest last. So surprise when arrive home, find SUV, parents in driveway.

Grandmother H drive car behind SUV, stop.

I open door, wave for parent attention. "What happen? Finish?"

Mother sign with much excite. "Victory! President quit. No new president, but board not make same mistake again. Not want more protest."

Father ask game.

"We win."

"Good day! Perfect." Father hug.

Jade, Grandmother H cook, bake.

Sit with Father, Mother. Talk long time. Parent tell protest story. Stop when Grandmother H say time for eat. Food good, but hurry eat. Want text Bradington friend good news.

Light flash in room. Look, see Father stand door. Father have note wrote for Grandmother H. "Jade show note. Jade say Grandmother H work all day learn sign say 'Good game.' Jade say you rude."

Father no understand.

"Mother understand. Shannon understand. Both know what like to live with hearing. You live family all Deaf. "

"I work all hearing," Father say.

"Work different. True family Deaf. Jade, Grandmother H not true family. Same M-U-G-G-L-E."

"Same what?"

Spell again, explain. "'Muggle' word from Harry Potter movie."

Tell Shannon story.

Father nod, but face show no true understand. Father live all life with family all Deaf. Not understand life grow up in family with hearing.

Father say, "Maybe story backward."

Look Father, not knowing meaning. Now my face show confuse.

"Maybe Jade wizard, you muggle."

Father close door.

JADE—I heard Dad come into the kitchen, but I didn't look up.

He tapped me on the shoulder. "Need make menu for week."

I nodded but kept on writing. When I finished the line, I pointed to the green construction-paper menu I was working on. "Funny, I make menu now. Menu for my restaurant."

"Have restaurant someday?"

I nodded. I liked putting menus together. This time I called my pretend restaurant Jade's Café. It would look like Emerald City in *The Wizard of Oz*. All green. Green booths, green plates, green glasses. The menu would be green, and all the entrees would have green names. Emerald soup. Avocado salad.

Dad looked at the menu I'd made. "All green food?" Dad asked. "Maybe serve green eggs and ham?"

Ha! I liked that idea. "Maybe name Jade's Place."

"Perfect."

"Lucky two grandmother good cook."

Dad nodded yes. "Last night food good," he said as he rubbed his belly. "Grandmother H good cooking."

"Grandmother G is a good baker. Perfect. Learn both. Two together make me great chef."

"Nice menu. You finish. I see what food Grandmother H bring."

I learned some new cooking things while Grammy was here, but I was happy Dad was home. Grammy and I talked while we cooked, and that was nice, but sometimes I'd get wrapped up in what I was talking about and forget to stir things. Dad and I don't need to talk. He points sometimes, and that's all he needs to do. Pointing at the onion means "chop it up." Sometimes he might sign "little" and I know that means dice, or he'll make a circle and that means slices.

Dad and I made the menu for the next couple of days, then heated up some leftovers for lunch. I flipped the upstairs hallway light from the foyer, and soon Marla came clomping down the stairs. She sat at the table, ate her food, and left without looking at me or saying a word.

I knew Marla was mad at me for showing Dad the note she wrote to Grammy. She called me a rat. I wanted to tell her if she didn't want anyone to see the note, she shouldn't have written it, but she turned her back on me before I had a chance.

After we cleaned up, Dad and I watched a baseball game on TV. During a commercial I told Dad that I was afraid I'd be sitting on the bench all season. I also told him that if I was playing with Tana's team—the team I was supposed to be on—I'd probably be a starting player now.

Dad said he was sorry. He promised next year would be different. And maybe I would learn more being with older, better players. The important thing was to try my best and have fun.

I didn't tell him it's hard to have fun when the coaches and most of the players don't even know I'm there. Maybe I'm so short they can't see me. Maybe I'm out of their field of vision.

I told Dad that Gretel thought I might be a good catcher. He nodded.

When the baseball game on TV was over, I called Tana. "We won our first game."

"Did you get a hit?"

"No," I said. I didn't tell her I sat on the bench the entire game.

"We won our first game, too! I got a hit! I didn't score a run, but I batted in two."

"That's nice," I said, but it didn't feel nice.

marla—Coach S tell me third base have idiom name "hot box." Name mean many difficult play happen third base. Baseball have many idiom. Make difficult communication. Coach S give book about baseball idiom.

Our team good team. Win four game. Lose no game. But game five maybe not win.

Claire—big, tall girl—not arrive for game. Twin say she go vacation with parent. Other catcher same away. No catcher. Big problem.

Gretel talk coach.

Surprise! See Jade wear catcher mask, catcher uniform.

Twin say, "Sister cute."

Cute not stop ball.

Coach say first day Jade job: play right field. Right field place for bad player. No understand how change.

Gretel arm around Jade. Gretel talk long. Gretel look, smile, fingerspell, "C-A-T-C-H-E-R-S R-U-L-E."

What catchers rule? Look up in baseball idiom book. No idiom about catchers rule.

I "lead-off batter." Name for first batter. I first because good. I must lead team for win. Must play good game today. Must play more hard, more better to make up for bad sister play.

JADE—We are losing. Down by three runs. We have no runs. No hits. Not because we have bad hitters, but because their pitcher is very good.

Gretel has done a great job pitching, but they've gotten three runs.

It is the bottom of the sixth and we have to start scoring. I am up next. Willow is in the batter's box. I'm standing in the on-deck circle.

Between pitches, I look over at the bench in the dugout.

Gretel mouths, "Catchers rule!" and I smile. We've been chanting, "Pitchers are cool, catchers rule" whenever we warm up.

I see Marla sign to one of the twins, "Need true catcher not here. Need good hitter."

I wave my hand to get Marla's attention. When she looks up, I sign, "You not get hit, too."

I turn my back on her so she can't respond. I chant, "Pitchers are cool, catchers rule" softly to myself as I wait for my turn at bat. Somehow, the rhythm of that little chant reminds me of "I'm No Hero." I stop chanting and start humming the melody.

"Strike three!" the umpire shouts.

Our batter goes down swinging just as I get to the refrain. I sing it aloud softly to myself. *"I'm no hero, but maybe I am . . ."*

Gretel is on deck now. Before I get to the batter's box she whispers in my ear, "She's tired. She's throwing low and slow. You are a catcher now. You see the ball differently. Watch the pitcher's hand. You know where the ball will go."

The pitch comes to me in slow motion. I hear nothing. I don't hear the crowd or the wind or the traffic on Maple Avenue.

Is this what it is like to be deaf? To be able to totally focus on the visual. Sound explodes into my ears. There is a huge *doink* as my aluminum bat hits the ball, followed by screams and cheers. I hear Gretel call, "Run!"

I put my head down and run. I don't look at the ball. I don't look at the girl at first base. I put my head down and dig it out.

I swear I hear the ball coming. I don't see it, but I hear it whistling through the air. It sounds so close. I don't look up. I look at first base. It gets closer and closer.

My shoe hits the bag.

I hear the ball slap the leather of the glove.

"Safe!"

It is the most exciting word I've ever heard.

Gretel steps into the batter's box. She is the last batter. Marla, the lead-off batter, steps into the on-deck circle.

Gretel looks at me and then up into the sky. I know exactly what she means: she's going to hit a pop-up. I'm to run.

I look at Marla and hopes she looks at me. She doesn't. I want to sign, "Throwing low." I wave my hand, hoping Marla looks my way. She sees me wave at her, but before I can sign "Throwing low" she turns her back on me.

Doink! Gretel hits the ball. She is running toward first base. I take a small lead off, but not too far. I watch the ball. As soon as the left fielder catches it, I tag up and run to second base. The left fielder must have bobbled the ball, because the third-base coach is screaming at me to run. "Take third!"

I watch the coach to see if he will tell me to slide. I don't need to. I'm safe. *Safe!*

Marla steps to the plate.

marla—Mother no go game because work. Father go game, drive home. Mother home now.

Jade happy. Run door.

Mother see Jade.

Jade no see Mother. Run stairs.

Mother face show happy.

"Good game? Win?" Mother ask.

"No."

Mother face show confuse. "Why happy Jade?"

"Jade think about Jade. Not think about team. Team lose, but Jade happy."

JADE—I ran to my room to call Tana as soon as I got home. I grabbed the phone from my desk and pushed speed dial, then fell back on the bed while I waited for the phone to ring.

The light flashed overhead. I heard that sick-cow sound from the door. Marla was standing at the door with one hand on her hip and her other hand still flipping the light on and off.

"What?" I said, without signing.

"No sit bed! Dirty. Shower. Change clean."

"Did you win?" Tana asked before she even said hello.

I turned my back on Marla. "No, but guess what!"

I didn't hear much of Tana's response because Marla was bellowing again. The light was going on and off.

When I turned to look at her at the door she was signing, "Off bed!"

I put the phone down, as I needed both hands to sign. "I'm off bed now, Bossy! Go! Get out of my room."

I pushed her out the door with one hand and shut the door with the other.

I put my desk chair in front of the door. Marla continued to pound on the door and bellow.

"Hello! *Hello!* Jade? Are you there? Is everything okay?" I heard from the phone on the bed.

"Sorry," I said, picking up the phone. "Just Marla being bossy again."

"So what about the game?"

"I played! I got a hit! I scored a run!"

I had to explain to Tana that even though I scored a run we still lost the game.

I was thirsty, so I trotted down the stairs to get a bottle of water out of the refrigerator as I told Tana how none of the other catchers showed up and I got to start. I was in the middle of telling her about a close play at home plate when I saw Marla signing to Mom in the family room.

I was sure I saw her sign, "Lose game because Jade!"

I dropped the phone from my ear. "What?"

"What? Jade? You still there?" I heard Tana's small voice say from my hand.

I raised the phone back to my ear. "Yeah. Hey, Tana—I gotta go. Call you back later."

I put the phone on the counter and took a long sip of my drink.

Then I stomped into the family room and pushed Marla aside. "Marla lie!" I signed.

Mom's eyes went wide with surprise.

Marla pushed me back. "No lie! Team lose because good catcher go vacation. Good bat not there."

"I get hit!"

"Only one hit. Other catcher maybe two, three, many hit."

"One hit better than you! You strike out! You no hit!"

I turned and ran up the stairs to my room. I slammed my door. Not that it mattered. No one would hear it anyway.

marla—Shower. Change. Father drive. Go twin house. Plan before lose. Plan celebrate fifth win. Lose because bad player for catcher. True catcher better hit. Baby catcher cause no win.

Twin no talk lose. Twin happy. Spend happy time together.

Twin share room. I sleep floor between bed. Three girl, one room. At school three girl, one room, but three bed. Go arcade. Bowl Skee-Ball. Play good. Win many time.

Before arcade twin decide we dress same. Comb hair same. People ask if triplet.

At home talk long time, no sleep.

"Maybe me sister same you," I sign. Point twins. "Maybe me triplet."

Twin nod. "Need tree name," Juniper sign.

Fingerspell O-A-K. "Oak good tree. Strong."

Willow face show disgust. "Oak not sound right."

Juniper nod. "Oak sound like boy."

Now my face show confuse. How sound like boy? Oak is tree.

"Juniper and Willow sound soft. Sound pretty," Willow explain.

"Like oak. Strong. Word short. Easy spell."

Willow face show excite. "I have idea! How about M-A-G-N-O-L-I-A?"

"What tree that?"

Juniper say, "Sounds pretty. Sounds like girl. Sounds beautiful."

"Not know how spell. Word sound same medicine name for when stomach hurt."

Willow get tree book. Point to tree. Pretty tree. Big, white flower.

"Magnolia perfect tree name," Juniper sign.

Like oak better, but say M-A-G tree fine.

Instead of spelling name we use J tree, W tree, and M tree.

JADE—My eyes popped open as the sun rose above the horizon. I reached over and flipped on the radio as the announcer said, "It's going to be a great day!"

Maybe I would win the secret song of the morning. Maybe Rob Bob would play "I'm No Hero" and I could dance.

Whatever happened, it would be a great day because it was starting without Marla! I got out my calendar and counted the days. She wasn't leaving for school for a month. That was exactly thirty-one days from now. It felt like forever. But at least I could enjoy today.

When the news came on, I plugged the speakers into my iPod, pushed "I'm No Hero," and cranked it up.

I pulled on a thick pair of sliding socks and grabbed another

pair for a microphone and did my "I'm No Hero" routine, then switched back to the morning program.

Rob Bob Phillips announced the secret song of the morning. I laughed at all the jokes, flopped back on the bed using Beezley as a big furry pillow, and sang along with the songs. Yup! Beezley had slept with me. It was almost like Marla was back at school. It was almost like Marla never existed!

Just when I thought it couldn't get any better than this, my phone rang.

"Jade, this is Mrs. Stob from next door."

I gulped. I didn't think my music had been loud enough for Mrs. Stob to hear.

"I didn't wake you, did I? I know it's sort of early."

"No! I'm an early riser."

"I was wondering if you could babysit for Amy this morning."

Amy is four and adorable. "Really? I mean, I'd love to! What time?"

"Starting at ten. Do you need to ask your mom or dad?"

"No. I mean, I'm sure it's fine with them." I'd taken a babysitting class in the spring and then passed out flyers to the neighbors. I had to ask permission to do that. Mom and Dad were fine with me babysitting.

"It's just for the morning. I should be home a little after noon."

I pulled my babysitting bag from the closet and took out the babysitting pad I'd gotten at the Safe Babysitter course. I wrote the date and the time. "See you then!"

My first babysitting job! I wished I could call Tana, but she was probably still asleep. Tana is not a morning person. I sent her a text instead.

marla

—Sad when twin mother take home. Twin perfect. Two sister who like me. Home have one sister who all time make problem.

Father in office. "Where Jade?"

"Not here. Babysit."

"Jade babysit? What for? Who?"

"Four-year-old Amy. Live blue house. Mother go meeting. Jade babysit."

Father work again. News to Father not special. Tap shoulder.

"Jade many babysit?"

"No. First time. Much excite."

Father work again.

Wonder why Mrs. Stob ask Jade. Should ask older sister, not younger sister.

Jade home soon. Face happy.

"Look!" Jade show twenty dollar. "I babysit Amy."

"Good, home. Hungry now. Lunch time. Make lunch."

"You babysit before?" Jade ask.

"Not important. Lunch important. Hungry now. Make lunch."

Jade go Father work room. Show twenty dollar. Father hug. Pat back. Not say lunch time.

When Jade leave Father work room, sign again. "Hungry. Make lunch now."

"Not lunch time. Lunch time is finished. I make lunch for Amy. I eat with Amy. Father ate lunch while I was babysitting. Make lunch for yourself."

"No! Your job. You make lunch for me. Make now!"

"I already made lunch. And I got paid to make lunch." Jade show twenty dollar again.

"You not responsible."

"I'm responsible. Mrs. Stob asked me because I'm responsible." Jade face show defy.

"Mrs. Stob only ask you because I not home."

Jade face show surprise. "Not true. Mrs. Stob call me on my cellphone. Did she call you first? No!"

"Mrs. Stob not know she ask baby to babysit baby. You need more responsible. Do job. Fix lunch now."

Jade face show anger. "Why ask girl who can't make her own lunch?"

"You talk talk talk—escape responsible."

Jade go kitchen come back with Quaker Oats box. "Here! Have your favorite for lunch." Put box in hand.

Jade go room. Jade runaway same rat again.

Father not know problem. I go Father work room.

"Jade no do job. Jade not make lunch."

"Jade work for Mrs. Stob, make lunch there. Maybe make soup for lunch. Easy. Open can, eat."

"Cook Jade job. Jade not responsible."

"Never fix food for yourself? Independence important. Same important responsible." Father look computer. Work again.

Stomach complain. Go to kitchen. Look for soup can. Look for can opener. Read direction on can.

Teacher say I independent. Teacher say I responsible. At school, I student leader. All teacher say. All student say. Father not understand how hard family for me because not all deaf. Father have deaf brother. Not hearing brother.

Remember calendar under bed. Thirty-one day until back to Bradington.

JADE—As soon as I got to my room, I called Tana. "She paid me twenty dollars!" I said as soon as Tana answered her phone. "Twenty dollars! I was only there two hours."

"Wow! What are you going to do with the money?"

I hadn't even thought of that. I was just excited about getting paid.

"I mean, are you going to buy something little now or are you going to save for something big?"

"Something big," I said, not knowing what that something big might be.

I told Tana how I'd taken my babysitting bag. Tana and I both made babysitting bags when we finished our babysitter safety course.

"Did you use the notepad?"

"Yeah, but all I did was write down her cellphone number and the time she wanted me to babysit. She said there was no need for me to know the name of the restaurant. She and her friend didn't know which restaurant they were going to go to anyway."

"Did you use the puppets?"

We had both put finger puppets in the babysitter bag. We had practiced putting little puppet shows together.

"I got them out, but she wasn't that interested. She wanted to play Chutes and Ladders. We played Chutes and Ladders about four times in a row. She cheats!"

"Did you let her?"

"At first. I didn't want to make her cry by calling her a cheater. I mean, what if she started crying or threw a fit?"

"I don't think you're supposed to let kids cheat. Ever."

"Well, next time. Oh, and get this. When I got back, Marla wanted me to fix her lunch."

"Why can't she make her own lunch?"

"Because it's my job . . . but I told her that Dad and I had already eaten. Then she said that the only reason I got to babysit was because she was spending the night with the twins."

"Did you tell her that hearing parents aren't ever going to hire a deaf girl to babysit their kids? I mean, what if something happened? She couldn't even call the mom on the cellphone. She couldn't even call 911."

"I know that and you know that, but Marla would never understand that. She lives in a Deaf world where the Deaf can do anything and everything. Saying something like that to her would make it seem like I hate Deaf people."

"But can't she see that parents would want someone who could hear? Someone who could communicate with their children? Someone . . ."

" . . . who could fix their own lunch!" we said in unison.

"Exactly," Tana said.

"No. She doesn't see that."

marla —Two games pass. Team win because baby player
Jade not play. Sit bench. Jade face happy. Jade, Gretel friend.

Gretel now Jade friend. Not my friend.

Going to game, Jade face show sad. Understand. Gretel pitch today. Jade not start player. Jade sit alone. Too bad Jade sad. Good. Maybe now chance to win.

Arrive game, Jade face show surprise. Coach give catcher uniform. Jade happy wear catcher uniform.

"What for? Why catcher play? Two other catcher here."

Jade look Father. Wave hand for attention. Sign to Father, "I'm not a backup! I'm a starter!"

Father smile big. Face show happy. Father must support daughter. But support daughter mean not support team.

Father, I talk many hour about game five. I know team lose game because Jade play. I explain Father that if better bat, better win. Not good bat. Maybe lose game again with Jade play.

Father say important support sister. Sister more important.

I team leader first. Must play for two Gilbert. Embarrass because sister bad play.

Last inning score same. Must score one run to win.

Tell twin, "Wish good catcher play. Maybe win."

Jade see signs. Face show angry.

"No angry. True."

Jade stand, sign angry, "I got on base."

"But not good hit."

"But I got on base. I didn't strike out like you!"

"That two game ago! Only game no hit. I leader. Lead team most hit. Two hit today! "

Sign big. Sign angry. Twin face show confuse. Coach face show annoy.

I must be leader, not have attention baby. Look away. Attention to game.

Next time bat, Jade not swing bat hard. Hit small. Same bunt. Run to first. Other team have bad defense. Safe.

Gretel hit hard, but not high. Ball roll low. Baseball idiom name: *Dribbler.* Jade run second base. Gretel out.

First pitch I hit ball hard, run first base. True hit. Run first base not because error same Jade.

Juniper hit ball next. Go far! I run second base. See ball on field, not player hand. Run fast. Run strong. Surprise to see Jade stand third. Why not run home?

Use voice. "Jade! Jade! Run! Run home!"

Jade not move. Jade stand. Two player one base mean out. Now run back, but second-base player have ball! Out! I move to third base. Tell Jade she need leave third base. Jade out because not run home.

Coach W point. Meaning: Go sit.

I sign Jade, "Coach say same. Sit."

Jade shake head. "No. Coach says you need to go to the bench."

Coach point again. Eye look me, not Jade. Coach want me sit? Not correct! Anger grow. Face flame hot. Sit, but know coach wrong.

Willow make next hit. Jade run home. Team win game. Jade think her play special.

All player run. Happy. Jump. All, but not me. Time for drive home.

JADE—This time I didn't have to wait to get home to call Tana. I brought my phone and left it in the SUV. She didn't answer. She was probably still playing her game.

I left a message. "We won. We won and I played. I started.

Even though the other two catchers were there, I started. I got a hit. I scored a run. I scored the winning run. Can't wait to tell you all about it. Call me the second you get this message."

We pulled into the driveway. Mom was home, so I could tell her the news. But those thoughts flew out of my head when I saw the suitcases.

There were suitcases sitting in the foyer.

"What? Go to Gallaudet again? More president problem?"

"No. Silly. Go family vacation. Father tell you. You never attention. Go pack things. Suitcase on bed. Hurry."

"Vacation?"

"Yes! Perfect time. Weekend no baseball practice. No baseball game. Go cabin in woods. Pack clothes for warm. Clothes for cold. Hurry. Leave soon."

Fifteen minutes later, we were out the door and I didn't even have a chance to call Tana to tell her I was leaving. I didn't even know where we were going.

When Marla gets in the car, she's fuming. Furious. She glares at me. I guess she's still mad at me because she was out. I don't know why she thinks it's my fault. And I don't care.

I pull a pillow from the back and shut my eyes and go to sleep. When I wake up we are somewhere in the mountains. No one is in the SUV. I rub my eyes, grab my bag, and go into the small cabin. First thing I notice is—there's no TV.

marla—Ask Father if Juniper, Willow come. Father say no. Vacation for family, not friends.

True. Jade sister, not friend.

Drive two hour. Many tree. No house. Road smaller, smaller, smaller. Last road dirt, not concrete. Get out. Stretch.

Cabin cute, but lonely. Only Mother, Father, Jade. Not even Beezley here. Beezley stay kennel.

First room: living room, kitchen together. Two bedroom. Bathroom. Must share bedroom with Jade. Put suitcase on bed next to window.

"I want bed next to window," Jade say.

I tell Jade. "First choice mine because older."

Jade throw bag on floor. Stomp away. Wish Jade stay in kennel not Beezley.

Sit bed. Text friends. Phone not work. Maybe battery dead. But green light. Confuse. Maybe broken.

Find Father on porch. Father sit chair. Feet up. Read newspaper. Drink pop.

Show phone. Father say, "Very far from town. Because far away, because mountain, no cellphone service."

"What?"

Father shrug.

"No TV?"

"No TV."

"What do?"

"Play game. Read. Walk. Mother bring many game."

JADE—"No cell service here?" I asked Dad.

Dad sighed. "Not dead if no phone friend."

"Tana doesn't know where I am."

"Fine. Fine, only weekend, not life."

"There's no TV!"

"Read. Play game. Walk. What you want do?"

"I want to call Tana and tell her about the game. I want to tell her about scoring the winning run."

Marla jumped in front of me, right between Dad and me. She startled me. I jumped back. I have no idea where she came from. I guess she was watching our conversation from the bedroom door. She had a crazed look on her face. She leaned forward signing big and fast.

"Lie! Willow hit winning run. You make error. You make me out!"

"What!" I said aloud, too stunned to sign. "No! You made yourself out," I told Marla.

"You not know play game. You should run home easy."

"I'm not as fast as you. Coach W say stop. Coach W say stay on third base."

"But I say run! You should run! You hear me! You hear me say run!"

"I heard you make noise. You sounded like a wild animal."

"No sound same animal."

"How do you know? You don't know what anything sounds like. You're deaf!"

"I know I not same animal."

"That's not the important part. The important part is I followed Coach W's instruction."

"Coach W wrong."

"On the team I listen to the coach, not my bossy sister."

Dad stamped his foot on the floor, and we both looked toward him. "Stop! Family vacation not for sister fight. For sister fun."

Marla crossed her arms in front of her and glared at me.

I raised my chin in defiance and glared right back at her.

"Stop," Dad signed. "Go! Walk! Friend say trail beautiful. Climb high. See far. Go. Walk. Be friend. Decide how not fight."

Marla stomped across the floor and out the screen door.

I dashed to my room, grabbed the half-full water bottle that I'd had with me in the car, and stopped in the living room to look around for my jacket. I couldn't find it. Dad waved his hand and I turned to look at him.

"Many trail. Important stay together. Hurry!"

I nodded and dashed after Marla, who had already disappeared into the woods.

"Wait! Wait up!" I screamed after her. Screaming at her was stupid, but somehow it made me feel better. There wasn't anyone around. I waved my arms big, hoping she would see me out of the corner of her eye. "Hey! Marla! You might want to take some water with you!"

I held up my water bottle and pointed at it as I tried to catch up with her. She walked on, totally unaware that I was struggling to keep up with her.

I cupped a hand around my ear. "What's that? No. You won't want any water at all. Fine by me! Don't complain when I won't share. I tried to tell you!"

The path was wide at first. The path kept splitting, and every time it split it got smaller.

How did she know this was the way? How did she know where she was going? She never paused. She just kept going up and up and up. I was panting and sweating.

I wanted to stop and take a drink from my water bottle, but I was afraid I'd lose sight of her if I did. I had no idea how to get back.

We climbed for about a half hour or more before I'd finally had it. I saw a boulder by the side of the path that was flat on the top and perfect for sitting. I sat down. I was so tired and thirsty I couldn't go another step.

Marla hadn't looked back once since we left, but the moment I sat down she turned around. Somehow she knew. "What for?" she signed. She was annoyed. It was as if this was a race and I was keeping her from winning again.

I took a drink and signed, "Do you know where you are going?"

She didn't answer. She just crossed her arms in front of her.

"How do you know which path is the right path? There are no signs."

"Dad say. You not good direction. You same Grandmother H. Bad plan."

Before I could respond, she turned and started up the trail again. I had to follow.

The trail was steeper and narrower, and I had a hard time keeping up. Sometimes she would look back and make a face when she saw how far behind I was. She'd stop, cross her arms, and look up at the top of the trees. As soon as I was within about three feet she would turn and continue up the mountain.

Finally we came to another large boulder. I sat down again.

This time it took a while for Marla to notice I wasn't behind her. She disappeared from sight, though I could still hear her crunching through the underbrush. The crunching stopped, and then I heard that sick-cow sound. She came back.

"Want water?" I asked. "You forgot water, so I will share. But only a little."

Her eyes narrowed and her lips twisted together in a tight knot. She didn't say anything, but stuck out her hand. I passed the water to her.

Marla was guzzling water down when I first heard it. I wasn't sure what it was at first. It sounded like the UPS truck when it turns from Washington onto Belmore. I realized we were far, far away from any road that would have a UPS truck. A second later I heard it again. This time it was louder, like a long, angry grumble. It wasn't a truck. It was thunder.

Marla tried to hand me the water bottle, but I didn't take it from her. Instead I put my hand out for her to stay still for a moment.

"Wait. Hear thunder," I signed.

Marla looked up at the sky. "Wrong. No rain. Sun."

"But hear thunder. Loud! Close!"

Marla tossed the water bottle at me. "Think not far now."

"You don't know! Maybe very far. I think we should go back now."

Marla rolled her eyes. "You baby worry. Walk far. Walk high. Finish first. Then home."

I had no choice but to follow.

The last part of the trail was very steep. I put the water bottle in my pocket because I needed both hands. I pulled myself up by grabbing onto roots of trees and big rocks. When I looked up, all I could see was sky.

The sky above us was blue and the sun was shining. But the thunder had changed from a low rumbling to a menacing growl.

It was so loud that I thought for sure Marla had felt it. She stopped and made a surprised sound—"Ahhhhhh!" Then she turned toward me, her face bright and smiley. "Beautiful," she signed. "Come! Hurry! Beautiful!"

I couldn't remember the last time Marla had smiled at me and said something nice. When I got close enough she reached out for my hand. I gave it to her, and she pulled me up the last few very steep steps.

From the clearing we looked out on the valley below. There were farms and woods and a road. A river wiggled through the valley. Sunlight glistened off the water.

I heard the thunder again. It wasn't low and grumbling anymore but more like dynamite exploding. I tapped Marla's shoulder and pointed to the sky behind us, just beyond a huge pile of rocks.

marla—Lightning. Strong. Bright. Big.

Two sky. One sky: sun, blue, happy.

Other sky: dark, mean, threat.

Sudden understand. Danger. Problem.

Jade no understand. Jade baby.

I older sister. Responsible sister.

Jade face show worry. "Come must go now."

Look wrist. No watch. But know. No time go cabin.

Look up. Tree move wild. Leaf fly from tree. Leaf make circle in sky. Leaf attack face.

At school, study science about weather. Study lightning knowledge, lightning safety.

Rain start fast. Many rain. Hard rain. Hurt head, face.

Jade find big tree. No rain under big tree.

Jade think tree idea good.

Jade baby. Jade no understand.

Lightning again. Again. Again. Lightning bright.

Thunder strong. Feel thunder in chest.

Jade face show afraid.

"No tree," I sign. "Tree bad."

No time explain maybe lightning hit tall tree. Lightning travel in root. Girl under tall tree maybe dead. See rock. Tall rock block wind, rain. Not cave, but rock attach same porch roof.

Rain fall. Knee, feet wet. Head not wet.

Tree dry. Jade point.

Tell Jade lightning knowledge from class. Jade nod.

Wet. Hair wet. Clothes wet.

Jade cold. Jade afraid.

Put arm around Jade.

JADE—The lightning was so bright that it hurt my eyes. It was so close I could hear it sizzle. The thunder was so loud even Marla heard it. Okay, maybe she didn't hear it, but she felt it. She jumped when it thundered. The ground shook.

We didn't say much because we had our arms around each other.

When it first started raining it was less like raindrops and more like pellets from a pellet gun hitting us on the top of the head and on our arms.

I ran toward a big tree. It was like a big umbrella.

Marla hooted, "No," and pulled my arm. She pointed toward a large cliff of rocks.

We couldn't sign to each other. It was hard to see. In the dark of the storm the lightning looked brighter, more threatening.

The big rock had a little overhang. It blocked some of the rain, but we were still getting wet.

"Look!" I pointed when we sat down. "Under tree dry."

Marla explained that it was a tall tree and that sitting under a tall tree during an electrical storm was dangerous. She said she learned it in science class last year. We would stay by the rock.

Every time lightning flashed I thought the tree might get hit by lightning and would burst into flame.

I was cold. I leaned up against Marla and she leaned up against me.

I looked at the path. It wasn't a path now. It was a stream flowing with water. Leaves were floating by.

Another bright flash of lightning. Thunder rumbled, but it sounded farther away.

I snuggled closer to Marla. She tightened her arm around me and we waited for the storm to end.

marla—No more lightning. Rain, but not big rain. "Go now," I sign to Jade.

Jade look up. "Maybe wait for rain to finish?"

"Silly! Wet. Rain same wet. Must go now. Home before dark."

Rain move leaves. Make hard see true way, but know must go right. Trail go down, go right.

Leaves make trail same ice.

Turn. Look Jade. Jade face show worry, afraid.

First sister responsible.

"Fine," I sign. "No worry. Know way. Walk careful."

Jade slide, almost fall. Face show afraid. Teach safety. Show hand on tree to stop.

Jade reach shoulder.

Jade want hand hold.

"Fine." Want say *Move slow*, but no say. Jade hold hand too tight. Tell Jade okay no need hold hand.

Walk. Then feet same bird. Feet fly to sky. World turn.

See sky, tree top before head hit ground.

Slide. Slide. Slide.

Many leaves.

Many stick. Poke leg. Poke butt. Poke face.

Put arm over face.

Slide fast. Slide dirty.

Then dark like sleep. Nothing.

JADE—It was getting dark. I don't know how long we walked. The trail was slippery.

Marla moved like an animal. I wondered how could she see where she was going. How did she know she was even on the trail?

When I finally caught up with Marla, I tapped her on the shoulder. She turned and I grabbed her hand. Marla looked at me and smiled. She gave my hand a double squeeze, then let go.

"No worry. Fine. Walk careful. Walk slow. Hand on tree make stop fast. Halfway down now. Not long. Soon warm. Soon dry. Soon food."

The way she said it so calmly made me feel better.

I nodded and smiled.

She nodded back at me and smiled.

Marla's next step sent her sliding. Her feet went up and she fell on her back. She slid off the trail and went down a small ravine. She made noise when she first hit the ground. Not the usual bellowing, sick-cow sound that she makes when she is annoyed and angry. The first sound was like air being knocked out of her. As she slid down the side of the ravine I heard little surprised grunts and groans as her body slid past small trees and rocks.

"Marla! Marla!" I called as I watched her slide.

Then she stopped. There was no sound. No grunts, no groans, no snapping of twigs, no rustle of leaves. It was quiet. The only thing I heard was the pounding of my own heart in my chest, in my ears. I called out her name again, knowing it was silly. Knowing she couldn't hear me.

I started climbing down the ravine very slowly. Reaching from tree to tree. I was using the trees like rungs on a ladder, trying to stay on my feet and not become a human sled like Marla.

Marla's eyes were closed when I got to her. She was lying still in a pile of wet leaves. Her eyes flickered open and closed, and she moved her head. She made a little moaning sound.

I put my hand on her hand to let her know I was there. She was not alone. I was there with her in the cold, dark, wet woods.

I wanted to cry. But I remembered the first-aid DVD I saw in my babysitter's course. I heard the woman's voice from the DVD. *Stay calm.*

"Stay calm," I told myself.

Assess the situation.

Was she breathing? She was breathing. Check.

To calm myself I started humming. I didn't even know what song it was until I got to the refrain. *"I'm no hero . . . but maybe I am."*

What was the next thing on the list? Was she bleeding? There was a smear of blood above her left eyebrow.

I brushed back Marla's thick hair. Her hair was wet and surprisingly warm. I looked at my hand. It was bright red. The sight of the blood brought a sick taste to my mouth. For a moment I thought I would throw up.

Oh, my God! She was bleeding!

Anywhere else? I checked her arms and legs and raised her sweatshirt to look at her stomach.

For bleeding we were supposed to put on a compress. At class the instructor said we could use a towel or a torn piece of clothing. I looked around like I might see a dish towel hanging from a branch. Nothing.

I took off my sweatshirt and then my T-shirt. I made a tiny tear in the T-shirt with my teeth, then tore off the bottom part.

My T-shirt was now a midriff. I put the top part back on, rolled the other section into a small square, and put it on Marla's head. I pushed down hard.

"Oww." Marla let out a hurt sound.

I eased off the pressure at first but then pushed down again. "Steady pressure," I told myself. I remembered that the lady on the video had said it was important to apply pressure to stop the bleeding.

"*Shhh!* Stay quiet," I said, smiling at Marla. "It's okay. It's okay," I kept mouthing to her.

I held the bandage on her head for what seemed a long time. Then I turned the bandage over and used the clean side to wipe away enough of the blood to see where it was coming from. There was a deep cut about an inch and a half long near the hairline.

"Can you hold?" I asked.

Marla started to nod but winced. Then signed yes with her hand.

What was next? Broken bones. I felt her arms and legs. Nothing seemed swollen or felt wrong.

Concussion. What had we learned about bumps on the head?

I did remember that it's important to keep injured people warm.

I wrung out my wet sweatshirt so it was as dry as I could make it. I laid it on top of Marla.

Marla put her left index finger on the spot right above the cut on her head and turned it out to me twice. It was the sign that meant, "What for?"

"Important you warm."

I did not sign "shock," but I knew shock might be a problem.

I tried not to move her.

I had no idea where the trail was, no idea how to get back. We were wet and cold. It was getting dark. I didn't want to leave Marla, but I had to go find help.

marla—Dark. Wet. Cold.

Feel warm hand on hand.

Move. Want sit.

Hand on chest now. Hand push down. Soft, not hard. Hand stay on chest.

Eye open. Eye close. Light hurt eye.

Hand move hair. Hand on forehead. Hand on face. Hand push. Owww! Head hurt.

Eye open.

See Jade face. Jade face, little smile.

Jade sign, "Stay. No move. Quiet."

Face study my face.

Jade look arms, legs. Hand touch. Jade pull sweatshirt up. Stomach cold.

"Hurt? Where hurt?"

Not know. Think. Think make brain hurt. Point to head.

Jade hand feel head. Feel bump back head. Ow!

"Night come soon. Must go for help now."

"No!" I sign. "No go!"

"No move. Stay quiet. Maybe hurt."

Wet leaf touch face. Jade move wet leaves.

Cold from wet leaves below same ice.

Jade take off sweatshirt. Use sweatshirt same blanket.

"What for?"

"Must stay warm."

Jade look cold. Rub hands on arms. Rub hands my arms.

"Must find help before dark."

"No go! You same Grandmother H. Always lost."

Look Jade eye. Jade face show understand. Show agree.

JADE—Marla gently pushed my hand away and sat up.

I held the compress on her head and tried to help her stand, but she started swaying like flowers in a swirl of wind.

"Ahhhh," she called out as she pushed her hand against me. She turned her body away and threw up.

The stench of the vomit hit me like a wall. I gagged, and for a moment I thought I was going to throw up too.

Instead, I focused on Marla. Her eyes rolled back in her head. I thought she was going to pass out. Gently I eased her back onto the ground.

I checked the rolled up T-shirt bandage on her head. It was bright red. It was completely soaked. I needed more bandages.

I took off my right shoe and sock. I turned the sock inside out and stuffed it full of leaves, hoping their coldness would help stop the swelling, stop the bleeding. And maybe the leaves would soak up a little blood too.

I put the new sock bandage on Marla's forehead and raised

her arm to hold it there. I kicked leaves over the vomit and hoped that would cover up the smell.

I took a look at the sock bandage and pushed hard on it myself. The cold from the leaves and the pressure seemed to be helping. Her gash wasn't bleeding as much.

I needed to go for help. I needed to go for help now.

marla—"Bad?" I point to head.

"No, small. But much blood."

"S-C-A-R?"

"Maybe, but small. Near hair. Fine."

"Maybe look like Frankenstein?"

First time Jade eye not show afraid. First time real smile.

"No. No, look like Frankenstein. Still beautiful."

"Think me pretty?"

"Not pretty. Beautiful!"

Surprise make eyebrow move apart. Face move make head hurt. Oww!

Jade change T-shirt bandage to sock bandage. Push on cut. Hurt at first, then feel numb.

Watch Jade face as she clean blood from face.

Then sudden head turn fast. Look left.

"Wait! Wait! Hear something!"

Want sit up see what Jade hear. But Jade hand on chest.

"No move. Quiet!"

Jade head turn. Look all way.

JADE—I swear I heard a car. And it wasn't far away.

My first instinct was to get up and run toward the sound. But the leaves were slippery. I'd have to move slowly, cautiously. And while I was thinking about it, the car had come and gone. There had to be another.

"I heard car. Maybe a road is close. I'll find the road. I'll find help."

"No go alone! "Marla signed back, her face in a grimace. "I go with."

She tried to sit up again. But I gently pushed her back down.

I thought she might have a concussion. I really didn't remember what to do about a concussion except keep the person lying down and still until help got there.

I put my sweatshirt back on top of her. I had to keep her warm. She might be going into shock.

"No leave. Shout! Maybe person in car hear."

"No, too far away. A person in a car would never hear."

I went to move away, and Marla grabbed my arm and squeezed hard. "No leave," she signed. Tears welled up in her eyes.

I couldn't remember the last time I saw Marla cry. I knew she must be very afraid. I nodded, and she let go.

"There it is again. Another car," I signed to Marla. "There must be a road just on the other side of that ridge."

I kicked leaves out of the way, searching the ground for a couple of rocks of a good size. I found a large flat rock and a not-so-flat one.

"New plan," I signed. I put a round rock in Marla's left hand. I put the flat rock under the rock in her hand. "Count ten, then tap three times rock on rock."

I put my hand on top of her hand and help her tap three times.

"Sound very loud. Echo through woods. I hear and know where you are!"

"This sound very loud?"

I nodded and made my eyes big. Deaf people read faces very well. I have to look like I believe this is true.

"I can hear the sound of the rock. The rock-on-rock sound is like a lighthouse. I'll hear the sound and follow it to where you are. Remember: count to ten and tap three times. Practice."

I silently counted as well. When I got to nine, Marla tapped the rocks together.

This would give her something to do, something to think about other than me getting lost.

"Must also hold bandage to head. Push down to make bleeding stop. Important. Push down."

Marla pushed down on the bandage on her head.

"Fine. Perfect. I will go find the road and come back. Maybe come back with help."

After clawing my way up and out of the little ravine, I went in the direction of the car sounds I'd heard. There was a small ridge that I climbed up and over. And there was the road. It was much lighter out on the road than it was in the woods. Maybe there was another hour or two of daylight left.

Good thing it had stopped raining.

But what I should do next? If I left this spot, I might not be able to find it again. Maybe I could build a little pyramid of rocks here, I thought. Or maybe I could tie something to a tree.

While I was looking around for something to tie, I heard it. A car was coming this way.

marla—...six, seven, eight, nine, ten. Tap! Tap! Tap!

Rock heavy in hand. Hand, arm tired. Other arm tired because hold head. Move bottom rock to other side of body. Move top rock from left hand to right hand. Move other hand to head. Wet sleeve on nose. Count again one to ten ... tap tap tap.

Hope Jade right. Hope road not far.

Try think, but think hurt head.

Shut eye. Remember Jade word. *Stay calm. No move.*

Tap many time. Count ten. Not count how many time tap. Tap many time right hand. Now right hand tired.

Move rock again left side. Count ten. Tap tap tap.

Surprise see something.

Animal maybe? Bear maybe?

No! Jade face! Jade plan good.

Hand touch arm. Touch face.

Hand warm.

Jade face show worry. "Okay?"

Head hurt. But sign, "Fine."

"Found road. Found woman with car. She's coming to help us."

No belief!

See woman face.

JADE—I was happy it was a woman in the car I flagged down. As soon as I started telling her my story—that we'd been hiking and caught in a storm and my sister had fallen—I burst into tears. She put her flashers on and got out of the car.

I told the woman my sister was hurt and lying down. I told her I didn't think she had broken any bones, but she had a big bump on the back of her head and a gash over her left eye. I thought she might have a concussion and didn't want her walking around. The woman followed me back to where I had left Marla.

I probably could have found her without the tap tap tap, but as soon as I heard it I felt better. I knew she was still awake and hadn't passed out.

Our rescuer, whose name was Patty, helped me sit Marla up. "Tank ooooouuu," Marla said, using her voice because we had her by both arms.

Patty's eyes got very wide. "What's wrong with her voice?"

"Oh, I forgot. My sister is deaf."

Patty and I pulled Marla to her feet.

Marla signed that she was dizzy and her right ankle hurt a little, but not so much that she couldn't walk, with help. Moving slowly and carefully with Marla between us, we managed to get out of the little ravine and over the ridge to Patty's car.

"Do you know where the cabin is?" Patty asked.

"Name road?" I asked Marla.

A pained look crossed Marla's face like it hurt to think, but she fingerspelled a name. "Bushkill Road?"

"I know where that is. It's not far."

When we got near, Marla tapped my knee.

"Marla thinks it's up here," I told Patty. I looked at Marla. "Which way?"

Marla pointed to the right.

"Go right," I said.

"Not far," Marla signed.

I didn't recognize anything until I saw the SUV, since I'd been asleep when we arrived at the cabin that afternoon.

Mom and Dad were both over near the trailhead, but when they saw the car headlights, they came running.

"Where?" Mom signed as she ran across the field toward us. "Where Marla?"

"Okay! Hit head," I signed back. "I find help."

Mom and Dad ran to the other side of the car to check her out.

"Your parents are deaf too?" Patty asked.

"Thank you," my dad said, using his voice.

Mom doesn't like having me talk for her. She prefers to use the pad of paper she always keeps in her purse, so I was surprised that she asked me to interpret for her.

Mom touched Patty's arm. She signed and then pointed to me.

"She said thank you for saving Marla. Thank you for bringing her home to me."

Patty looked at my mother and spoke. "You're welcome—I was happy to help. But your daughter is the real hero." She put her arm around me and patted me on the back.

I signed back the first part, the "you're welcome and happy to help," but not the hero part.

I'm no hero, I thought to myself, and the words from the song came to my head. *But maybe I am.*

Dad went to the cabin and came back with paper to ask for her address.

"Address please. Want send reward."

Patty wrote her cellphone number instead. "No reward. Just call to say if Marla is okay."

We all waved good-bye to Patty.

marla—In hospital, much wait.

Ask Jade where learn first aid. Learn Jade take first-aid course when learn babysit.

Jade tell about babysitting class.

Doctor say lucky. No broke bone. No sprain. Maybe small concussion. Cut on head need four stitches. Lucky sister know first aid.

Finish hospital. Very hungry! Stop McDonald's. Jade say what want from drive-thru. Many time not use drive-thru, not make order through speaker.

Eat in car on way back to cabin.

JADE—I didn't realize how muddy I was until I got back to the cabin. I looked in the bathroom mirror and realized I had mud in my hair, on my legs, everywhere. There was a big smear above my right eyebrow. Good thing we hadn't gone into McDonald's.

I took a quick shower and was exhausted. I fell asleep but woke often. It seemed every time I closed my eyes I was back in the same dream. A dream with thunder, lightning, cold, wet, and the smell of vomit.

In my dreams I would hear Marla moan. Sometimes I'd wake up and she would really be moaning.

I got up several times to get more ice to put on the bump on her head. At two a.m. I got up to give her more pain medicine.

When I woke her again at six for more medication, Marla was not happy. At two she'd responded very well. She took the pill from my hand, took the glass, swallowed the pill quickly with a gulp of water, and went right back to sleep.

Six a.m. was a different story. Her eyes fluttered open and she glared at me.

"Go away. Teen need sleep."

She shut her eyes and I had to shake her shoulder again. "Take pill, then go back to sleep."

"Light hurt eye. Make window dark."

I put a blanket over the window and then shook her arm again to wake her up to take her pill.

If looks could kill, I'd be dead. Apparently it would take more than a bump on the head to knock the bossiness out of Marla.

At ten I woke her again. I asked if she was hungry and she said yes, so I brought her breakfast in bed. It was only toast and orange juice.

She took one sip of the orange juice and made that sick-cow noise again. "Take away. Hate!"

"What? Why?"

Marla made a face and fingerspelled P-U-L-P. "You know I have hate for P-U-L-P. Always do for annoy. Take away. Toast dry! Want tea!"

I almost asked her if she was sure she didn't want coffee, since she was the grown-up teen now. But I said nothing. I took the orange juice and went to make tea. Her words echoed in my head. *Always do for annoy.* Tears stung my eyes. Honestly, I had no idea that she didn't like pulp. Besides, I wasn't the one who bought the orange juice. Mom did. I was only trying to help.

I brought in the tea. "Be careful. Hot. Don't spill. Maybe need to sit up."

"Rude! No tell me be careful. Not baby."

I stomped from the room and resisted the urge to slam the door.

I returned to get the tray only when I heard her breathing hard and knew she was asleep. I took the breakfast dishes back to the kitchen.

I let Mom take her lunch and dinner. The day was rainy and cold. I played Qwirkle with Mom and Dad.

I was worried that Marla was sleeping too much, but Mom said that sleep was good. It would help her heal, help her to feel better faster.

But would it make her any more enjoyable to be around?

marla —Stay in bed all Saturday. Sunday morning get up, move to living room couch.

Jade bring extra pillow. "Maybe this help. Maybe this feel comfortable."

"Fine. No need you. Go away!"

Jade face show hurt.

Father suggest play game. Good idea. Qwirkle not good because hard to reach table from couch bed. Play card game instead. Jade my partner. Beat parents three time.

Jade give high five. Face show worry. "Sorry. Hit too hard? Okay? Feel okay?"

"Stop ask okay all time. Rude!"

"Sorry. Do you need another pillow?"

"Stop! Treat same baby. Not baby! You annoy. Same bug."

Jade eye have tear.

"Now cry same baby!"

Jade go room.

Father face show anger.

"Jade very good nurse. Give pill. Bring food. Make comfort."

"But annoy! Ask all the time: 'Okay? Okay? Okay?' Not baby!"

"Jade worry for you."

"Baby worry. Doctor say fine."

"Fine because Jade know first aid."

"But ask all time! 'Okay? Okay?' Many time annoy. Make me feel same baby."

"Maybe now know what like to be younger one. Maybe now know what feel to always be treated like baby by older sister. I know. Older brother do same."

Forget Uncle Andrew older. Forget Father is little brother.

Mother come living room from bedroom. "Look! Sun out! Maybe beautiful view."

"No time hike," Father sign. "Leave soon, must lunch first."

Jade say, "No problem. I make lunch and watch Marla. You both can go on a hike, but don't fall!"

I start sign, not need Jade watch me like babysit Amy next door, but Father wave hand. Meaning: Stop, don't speak.

"Marla feeling better," Father sign. "Maybe Marla help fix lunch."

Now my face show surprise.

"You feel better, right?" Father ask.

Jade face show worry.

Father say, "No worry. Marla help make salad maybe. You teach. Marla learn from best. Marla need learn cook. Cook important for independent."

JADE—I showed Marla how to take a head of lettuce and slam it on the counter so the core slips out easily. I showed her how to clean carrots with a vegetable peeler. She made the salad while I made spaghetti and heated up spaghetti sauce.

"You nurse someday?"

"Nurse? No! Hate seeing blood. I almost passed out!"

"Why nurse for me?"

I looked at her surprised. "You're my sister!"

"If not nurse, what do?"

I blushed. I was a little afraid to tell her what I really wanted to do because she might make fun of me.

"What?"

"Maybe cook. Maybe baker?"

"Restaurant?"

"Yes. Maybe own restaurant or bakery."

Marla looked surprised now.

After lunch, Dad helped me clean up. We packed everything and left.

I was still awake by the time we were about an hour from the cabin and an hour from home. It's easier to stay awake when you have someone to talk to.

Marla was into a big story about this boy that her roommate Tabitha likes when she suddenly let out an excited yell. She dug in her pocket for her cellphone. "Text! Cellphone work again!"

I pulled my cellphone out of my bag and turned it on. There were thirty-six text messages, all from Tana. I didn't bother reading any of them. I just punched in speed-dial and her phone started ringing.

"Where have you been? I thought you were kidnapped or something!" Tana screamed into the phone without even saying hello.

"Oh, my parents wanted to go to some cabin in the woods for the weekend," I said.

Marla was pulling a pillow from the back seat and putting it up against the window. I reached out and tapped her on the leg. "Wait, almost finished," I signed to her.

Tana was telling me she almost freaked out when she couldn't get hold of me.

"Tana, I can't talk now," I said. "Can I call you later?"

"Okay . . . but you better call. You still haven't told me about the game."

"Oh, yeah, the game!"

I hung up the phone. It seemed like weeks, maybe months, since I had played that game. After our four days in the mountains, it didn't seem as important. I'd almost forgotten about that fight Marla and I had had before we went for the hike.

I put away the phone. "Finish," I signed to Marla. "Tell me more."

"What?"

"Story about Tabitha and boy."

"Really? Want hear story, not talk Tana?"

I nodded.

Marla smiled and started again with the story, then paused.

"Wait! Wait Father look mirror."

She reached forward and playfully slapped Dad on the shoulder.

Mom asked, "What for?"

"Father no spy on conversation," Marla signed to Mom. "Talk for sister, not talk for parent."

Dad put his hands in the air in a surrender gesture. Mom moved the rearview more so Dad couldn't watch our conversation.

Marla moved her hands closer to the back of Dad's seat so it would be harder for Mom to see what she was signing. She told me about a boy she liked named Jimmy.

"You have boy *you* like?" Marla asked me.

I didn't say anything, but my checks burned like they were on fire.

"What name?"

I look at the front seat to make sure no one was looking back and then fingerspelled S-K-Y-L-A-R. But I didn't think he liked me, I told Marla.

"You need strong," she signed. "You need confident. Stand tall. Fill with Gilbert pride."

I nodded, but my face must have given away that I wasn't very sure.

"Not worry, text me." She held up her phone. She put her hand on my knee. "I help."

I wasn't sure if Marla could text me confidence. But I liked the idea. It was worth a try.

marla—Doctor say not play baseball until Thursday. Not wear uniform. Team friend face show surprise.

"Marla! What's wrong? Why no uniform?"

Gretel make okay sign. Face show worry.

"Sick?" twin signed same time.

Put hand out. Meaning: Stop question. Sign, "Game start fast. No time talk. Time for practice."

See Jade put on catcher front, catcher face.

Wave hand for Jade attention. "What! Start again?"

No see Jade face. Catcher face hide. Jade move. Jade smile.

"Yes! Start again! Not mascot! I'm a real player."

Jade move catcher face again, turn, look Gretel. Jade think mascot? Why? Why not think player?

Think, think, think while watch team prepare game. Practice throw. Practice catch. Understand grow. Jade problem: no confident.

Game start. Team defense first. Jade behind home plate.

Fast understand. Jade small. Jade young. Other player older, bigger. See first time why no confident. See first time that Jade brave . . . like mouse play on team with lion.

Watch game hard because team leader sit, not play. Need be leader from sit.

Wave for Jade attention. Jade move up catcher face, look. Sign, "What?"

"Have sister pride! Must play hard! Play for two sister!"

Jade face show surprise, then pride. Jade nod. Move catcher face down.

Between inning many time to talk with friend about why not play.

Tell many time story of walk, woods, lightning, fall, hurt.

Willow, Juniper face show worry.

I sign, "Fine. Head fine. Hard like rock. Maybe rock hurt more."

Juniper ask if still have bump.

"Can still feel bump, but little now. Not hurt when touch. Lucky head hard."

Willow, Juniper both nod, say same time, "Lucky you were not alone."

Willow sign, "Lucky that Jade was with you."

Juniper sign, "Lucky that Jade knew what to do."

Gretel sign, "Lucky that Jade heard the car."

Last out fourth inning. Team players stand. Run field.

Think about Gretel words. *Lucky Jade hear car.* Never thought before, but Gretel right. Lucky have hearing sister.

Team play well. But last inning start, other team three hits. Each base have player. Batter very big. Or maybe look big because catcher Jade very small.

Big girl hit ball. Ball go far. Maybe home run. Willow chase ball. Willow throw ball. Juniper catch. Throw ball to home. Jade put block home. Ball come. Big girl come.

My heart beat hard.

JADE—The bases were loaded when a huge girl shuffled to the plate. I put my fist in the center of my glove and twisted my hand around as if to make room for the pitch. I crouch down and extend my arm. My eyes locked with Gretel's eyes.

One more out. All we needed was one more out and we'd win.

But if giant girl here hit a home run, it was all over—we'd lose the game. And just as I had that thought, Gretel threw the pitch.

There was a loud crack, and *zoom*, the ball took off for center field. It looked like it might clear the fence. Willow backpedaled, jumped, just missed the ball, and fell to the grass. The ball hit the fence and bounced back into the outfield. Willow jumped up and chased down the ball.

"Throw it! Throw it!" I screamed as the player who had been on third crossed home plate behind me, closely followed by the player who was on second. The girl who'd been on first base was rounding third. The batter—giant girl—was halfway between second and third.

The throw was in the air. Willow threw to her sister at shortstop. Before Juniper caught the ball, the girl who'd been on first base crossed home plate. But giant girl wasn't all that fast, and I was sure she'd stop at third. Well, I *hoped* she'd stop at third, but I couldn't be sure. I put my glove out. "Throw it! Throw it!" I said under my breath.

I was ready. I put my body on the baseline like I'd been taught. I put my arm out, ready to catch the ball. "Look at Juniper, not at third base," I told myself through gritted teeth.

I didn't have to look—I could hear her coming. Her steps were as loud as the thunder in the woods.

I swear I could hear her shoes creak as they hit the dirt. I swear I could hear dirt being pulverized into dust. I looked at Juniper. I saw her throw. The ball zinged from the mound to the plate. I didn't take my eye off the ball even though I could feel the momentum of something big and very heavy moving my way. I saw only a shadow. Like a charging bull, like a speeding train, something big and fast and scary was coming my way.

I felt the ball in my glove. My body blocked the plate. The world went white. There was no noise.

In an instant I felt the crush of weight against me. I felt like I was falling. In my mind, I saw myself back in the woods, falling down the ravine. I was lying on dry ground, and trees were falling on top of me.

"Marla," I called out, but there was nothing but silence and dust.

marla—Big girl hit Jade!

Jade small. Jade same bug under big foot.

No see umpire call safe or out. Not know. Not important. Worry for Jade.

Jump! Run! Voice escape throat, "Jade! Jade!" Throat hurt from yell.

Jade eye close.

Put hand on Jade hand. Want Jade know Marla here. Jade not alone.

Jade eye open, close. Same butterfly.

All team around small player Jade.

Jade mouth word. Maybe "Owww!" Maybe say "Hurt."

Gretel say, "Yes!"

Willow, Juniper say, "Yes!"

"What? What Jade say?"

"Jade ask if the runner was out!" Willow fingerspell to me.

Know now what do for first aid. Jade taught. Breathing? Yes.

Bleeding? No. Broken bones? Where hurt? Ask Jade.

Jade point to head.

Win game important, but Jade okay more important.

Feel head. Head small bump. No blood. Help Jade to bench. Jade sit close. Put Jade head on my leg. Hold ice on head bump.

After game Father, Mother look Jade head.

"Okay! Fine! Both Gilbert sister, strong. Both have hard head." Knock on head same knock on door.

Father sign, "Hard head better than hard heart."

My eye meet Father eye.

JADE—As I climbed the stairs, I heard the sound of packing tape being applied to boxes. I paused at Marla's door. She was focused on taping boxes closed. I flipped the light switch to let her know I was at the door. "Need help?"

Marla shook her head no. "Almost finish." She leaned forward to drag another box closer so she could tape it shut.

I waved my hand to get her attention. "Father says to tell you we leave in one hour."

Marla nodded and immediately focused back on the boxes in front of her.

I couldn't believe Marla was going back to Bradington in an hour! The last week was a blur. It seemed like the game where I got body-slammed by Godzilla was months before, except that I could still feel the bump on my head. But just barely.

Marla held ice on my head for the rest of the game and all the way home in the car. I wasn't dizzy. I didn't feel sick to my stomach. It was only a tiny bump on the head. It didn't keep me out of the next game, but I didn't start because Gretel wasn't pitching. That time I got to sit on the bench and cheer for Marla. We won!

We ended the season 11/1. We had our team banquet at Cici's Pizza. I won Most Improved Player. Marla got Most Valuable Player.

I put the trophy on my dresser. It's the first thing I see when I enter my room. *Jade Gilbert, Most Improved Player.* Every time I see it, it makes me smile.

Back in my room while Marla finished packing, I was surprised to find Beezley on my bed. It was as if he knew Marla was leaving and he was ready to move back in with me.

When I turned on the radio, "I'm No Hero" was on. I kicked off my shoes just in time to slide. Unfortunately, I slid away from my dresser, so I didn't have time to grab a pair of rolled-up socks. I used my fist instead as a microphone. When I slid the opposite way, the light flashed overhead. Instead of looking toward the door, my head instinctively turned toward the clock. It was two in the afternoon. Marla had better not complain about elephant feet or horse dancing at two p.m., I thought.

I turned, ready for a fight. I was surprised to see Marla standing at the door with her softball trophy in her hand.

"Not taking your trophy to Bradington?" I asked.

"No. No, leave here. Stay with you. Stay your room."

I couldn't hide the puzzled look on my face. A month ago that puzzled look would have made Marla angry, but now it made her laugh. She put the trophy in my hand and nodded at me to look at it.

I looked down at it. Marla had put first-aid tape over her

name. On it, in tiny, neat letters, she had written *Jade Gilbert*. She'd left the words *Most Valuable*, but over the word *Player* she had put another piece of first-aid tape, this time with the word *Sister* written on it.

I gave her big hug, careful not to hit the back of her head with the trophy.

"That dance for favorite song?" Marla asked.

The song was over now, but I nodded.

"What song name?"

"I'm No Hero."

"Good words?"

"Yes. The best!"

"Hmm. Need song for talent show. Maybe this good song."

"I can teach!" I said. I was excited because signing songs means taking the signs and exaggerating them into beautiful movements. I would love to see how Marla and her roommates would sing "I'm No Hero." But right now I was going to teach Marla the dance that Tana and I invented.

I dove across the bed for my iPod. I punched up the song, put the iPod in the speaker stand, and rushed back to end of the bed. *"Don't wear an S upon my chest . . ."*

marla —Weekend finish. Now time for parent, Jade leave.

Jade face show sad. Surprise see tear. Hug Jade big.

"Fine, Jade. See fast. See one week. Five day."

Jade face show excite. Get Christmas cookie box from bag.

Put dresser. "For you," Jade sign. "Don't look at it now. Look at it after I leave."

Parents many hug. Hug for roommate same.

Wave good-bye from window. Family gone. Time with friend start.

"Surprise see Jade sad," Tabitha sign.

Jasmine nod. Sign, "Same."

Explain why feel close now. Jade nurse time make heart tender.

"What box for?" Jasmine ask.

"Hope cookie!" Tabitha say.

Open box. Cookie smell make room smell good. Laugh when see picture on inside lid.

"What?" Jasmine ask. Take lid from hand. Jasmine face show confuse. "What for?"

Jade cut oatmeal man from box. Put on inside lid. Write words: *Because oatmeal is your favorite!*

Letter inside.

Dear Marla,

Miss you already! I made oatmeal cookies, because I know oatmeal is your favorite. Ha ha! Half the cookies have butterscotch chips. Half the cookies have raisins. Text me which one you like better and I'll make more.

Jade

P.S. Here are the words to "I'm No Hero."

"Good! Perfect!" Tell roommate about hero song. "Think perfect for talent show."

Roommate look song words. Nod.

"Good also for dance. Jade make dance for hero song. Show how dance look with words. Show song two time."

Roommate love song. Want learn word. Want learn dance.

Before teach feel phone vibrate. Look, see who text from. Surprise show on face.

"Who?" Tabitha ask. "Friend from baseball?"

"Never guess!" I tell roommate.

Jasmine ask, "From boy?"

"Yes, boy!"

Jasmine, Tabitha eye grow big.

Laugh. "Tell true . . . boy dog!"

Jasmine, Tabitha face show confuse.

Text say: *This Beezley. Very sad UR not home. Sleep w/Jade but only because Jade sad. Count days until U return.*

Reply: *Miss U Beezley. Protect Jade no more bump on head. Count days also. Tell Jade I love her.*

CPSIA information can be obtained at www.ICGtesting.com
Printed in the USA
LVOW121615111212

311162LV00003B/76/P